Sarah -

I hope you enjoy a trip to TWO -

Many of the things + occur in the story really occured! Fun!

Blessings

KA

TWO-JAY

TWO-JAY

A Novel

Kent Turner

Copyright © 2023 Kent Turner

Library of Congress Cataloging-Publication- Data

Turner, Kent

TWO-JAY / Kent Turner- 1 st ed.

ISBN 979-8-35090-108-5

This work is sincerely dedicated to Jack, Mickey, Julie and the rest.

In whom we each find a piece of ourselves. Most of all to Connie, who is

my Michaela, my Julie and all other women, and for whom I wish I could

be Jack.

~ Author's Note ~

Life, as most of us have experienced it, is often stranger than fiction. Many of the events in this work were inspired from real life. Like in our lives, the fictional town of Redlands contains people. It's those people of a community whose love and dedication, challenge and hardship, success and... that which is the opposite of success; however we define it, that make up the brief moments of our lives. Those moments that we each experience while we breathe, move and have our being, are made to be their most valuable when we keep a sense of humor.

Kent Turner

At home in Oklahoma, 2022

Contents

TWO-JAY

Redlands

On the range, the low hills that lined the eastern edge of his land lay in the background as they walked with the wind on their backs. Moving westward, just above the stir of the light wind he could hear the bees moving from one field bloom to another. Sometimes only inches away from the hooves, they barely moved as the palomino stepped steadily forward. It was the best part of the ride, the range and the quietness. Clumps of stranded wheat left in place from the turning of the combines at the edges of the fields, speckled them with amber in otherwise barren tracts of tilled land. As he gradually moved off the range to the well-traveled path near the tracks, they trod together the familiar path to the township of Redlands.

The CO-OP, staffed now on Saturdays only during springtime and harvest, left the south end of Grain Street deserted late on the last day of the week. The Double-J Ranch, or Two-Jay as it had become known to almost everyone, lay twelve miles to the southwest. It still remained narrowly connected to town if one traveled by horse, by a worn down trail of railroad easement. Only fifteen minutes by pick-up truck, Jackson D. Gentner and his equine partner, together often made the journey at a slower pace. The route required an additional hour, but returned the effort. They were rewarded by a fine life. Though section lines crisscrossed the county, his ranch remained a personal outpost of a satisfying life born over a century earlier by his grandfather's father. As he stroked the neck of his companion, the two gradually transitioned from the soft trail onto the broken asphalt that only a mile further would become the officially named street leading into Redlands.

As the town closest to Two-Jay, Jack always took the slow route when time didn't matter so much. With only two-thousand eight-hundred residents, shopping for most was easy enough. But as things stood, it lacked certain essentials that had to be gathered in a pick-up or small stock trailer at the larger but more distant city of Carson. Thirty-three miles to the south, Carson stood as the County Seat. As he strode into Redlands, his six foot, lean frame fit the strong Quarter Horse well.

Today's errand, just a few boxes of welding rods, could easily be carried in a bag near the flank of Reacher, his sixteen hand palomino. Late on Saturday they moved unopposed down the pavement. Just under four years young, Reacher's stable mentality and well trained, if short life, made him ideal for Two-Jay, and for Jack. A half dozen other horses stocked the Two-Jay. The only other prime mount being Jupiter, who belonged to his co-owner, who as life had determined it, was also his sister.

Juliana, or Julie as most people knew her, at twenty-eight, sat a good horse and could barrel race with the best of them. Five-feet seven inches of her all told, two feet of her most frequently remained covered by a braided mane of her own which hung down her back. Ash brown hair in summer; it had always been made so by the sun. Her strong but managed figure always looked appropriate together with Jupiter, her Paint Horse. Since childhood, family photos etched in her mind the necessity for a paint. Hardworking as she was, no other seemed to befit a woman who earned her daily necessities off of the land.

Reacher snorted as they came to rest at the CO-OP. The business existed primarily for farming and ranching. And it would only be open for ten more minutes. Jack and Reacher had come part way at a lope in order to make it on time. The central stretch of the worn path paralleling the old Santa Fe railroad bed was smooth and free of hazards, allowing them to move quickly for miles. As Jack tied Reacher to the gas pump nozzle he relaxed, knowing he could start Monday's tasks with what he needed already on hand. Few people were going to come to this end of town this late on a Saturday to buy gasoline. The people that were in town at this time were there mainly either to buy their groceries or eat at the only real restaurant in town, the steak house.

"Fill up Reach," Jack said, roughing the withers of the muscled animal. Reacher swung his head in Jack's direction as his companion turned on the hose by the pump. Running water into a bucket kept there mainly for horses, it was also sometimes used to clean windshields and needed washing thoroughly.

"MIKE?" Jack called, his voice producing a small echo from the inside of the garage.

A heavier man in his late thirties with combed back brown hair and dirty blue jeans came around the corner of the building.

"Hey Jack, we have your rods in there on the table, three-eighth's inch, same type. You can go get em' while I say hello to Reach here!"

"Good, Mike. Thanks for getting them in so fast. We have some trailer and corral work to do."

Jack hurried toward the side of the building as Mike turned back quickly to catch him before he rounded the corner, out of voice range.

"Hey Jack, is that pretty sister of yours out there all alone today?" Not stopping to converse, Jack didn't slow down. He even increased his speed, skipping up onto the sidewalk that circled the building. "All alone Mike!" came the only reply.

The weighty attendant rubbed the coat of the handsome horse. "If I had any sense Reach, I'd be out there while Jack is here. Julie is even prettier that you are!" He gave the tall, golden Quarter Horse a pat on the rump while walking around the fuel pumps thinking audibly. "He's got everything Reach; Julie, you and the best three-hundred-eighty acres in the county." Shaking his head, Mike pulled the station keys out of his pocket, ready to lock-up.

He followed his thoughts, now reminiscing about the days of high school and attending Redlands schools with Jack, Julie and thirty others that still lived in the area.

JJ

"Well you ought to at least consider it," Julie said, while removing the dinner plates and a platter full of stuffed potatoes, beans and homemade bread from the dinner table.

"I don't know, this place keeps the two of us busy even with the seasonal people that we hire," Jack said.

"Fine!" She tossed the dishtowel into the sink full of water. After years of hard work, the two shared the benefits of comfort that they had earned. Only the two of them shared in the family house. And being able to afford what creature comforts they desired, they still washed their dishes by hand. It was habit. They had done so since they were kids. She continued the conversation in frustration from the kitchen, speaking loud enough to ensure that he could hear her.

"Okay fine... You don't want to meet her, you don't have to; but I'll tell you this Jack; you are thirty four. Think about having kids of your own someday. How old are you going to be when you do? Sixty? Oh, that will be fun for the kid, helping dad put in his

17

dentures and his diapers huh? You know, those pull-ups are awfully messy when you are riding the ranch. What a lucky kid!" She said. Chewing a mouthful of the bread ground from last season's grain, Jack sighed and looked down into his plate. How many times were they going to discuss this? Since their parents were gone, Two-Jay had been theirs, just hers and his; brother and sister. He called back to the kitchen.

"Look Julie, would you mind too much if I just finish this in peace? I mean it's pretty good bread and beans you made, but it loses a lot with too much advice."

"Oh!" The only verbal sound came from the kitchen, as the refrigerator door had been slammed hard. He heard her footsteps trail off in the direction of the bathroom. Jack looked at his plate and then raised his head sighing while staring at the wall. The picture of Julie and he from when they were in 4-H together twenty years before, sharing a work project still hung at eye level. It was beginning to yellow these days, like her advice on marriage. He pushed his chair back and stood, leaving the plate half full for the moment. He found her in the bathroom with the door open, washing her face.

"Okay, maybe you have a point. If you really think it's a good idea, I'll meet her, okay?"

"You mean it?" Julie asked with her eyes closed, washing the soap off her face as lengths of her brown hair fell into the western style sink.

"Sure! I don't know, maybe we would hit it off. Who knows?"

He picked up the face towel and handed it to her, moving back to stand in the doorway as she wiped her face dry. She turned to face him. Even at twenty-eight, after years of hard work and play in the sun, his sister was pretty. Not having sincerely looked at her lately, he had to admit, Mike had been right about her.

"Thanks Jack," she said, turning to hang the hand towel up neatly as he straightened up to go.

"Besides; if I don't find a girl, I'll be stuck living with you for the rest of my life. What a thought!" Laughing, he gave his sister a hard swat on the butt that was sure to sting, swatting harder than he usually did when he smacked Reacher. He left the bathroom smiling to finish his dinner. "There you go!" came the reply from her bathroom.

"And I'll tell Mike at the CO-OP, you are ready to date!" He called, laughing loudly as he sat back to finish his plate with a renewed appetite.

"And I'll castrate you in your sleep!" came the last reply, as her bedroom door thumped shut.

J J

At two-thirty, they pulled into the driveway after the twenty minute drive from town. The steakhouse, nearly always full with church over, wasn't the quietest place to eat. Their family history

19

had always held to being in church on Sunday morning, except on occasion during calving. About three-hundred of the town's population ate at the steakhouse on Sunday. It had been a good meal, and he had enjoyed the company. Julie had introduced him to her friend from Ag. school whom she'd known years before. The three had lunch, spoke both politely and pointedly, and made small talk after eating. Still at the table as the last of the noontime crowd began to leave, the noise of conversation died down. They discussed the basics of interests, experiences and goals.

"Seems nice enough," Jack spoke audibly at home, as they walked from the truck to the house.

"I think so too. And she is really smart. She was a vet-tech before deciding to go into cattle full time," Julie replied.

"It would be nice to have another full time partner at auction time," he joked.

"Uuugh," Julie muttered, frustrated as she moved through the house to her room.

Jack stepped outside, still in his Sunday jeans and shirt. Walking out to the barn and inside to the corner of it, he beheld an antique thresher from the early nineteen hundreds. Examining a shaft that needed a race and bearing, but too worn otherwise without being rebuilt, he thought about it. A longer term project, he enjoyed working with it. He overcame an urge to get his

20

hands dirty in the grease and thought about the girl they had shared lunch with over an hour earlier at the steakhouse. Jack pictured her in the kitchen; cooking, smiling and being a wife. He shook his head. "Hmmm... not ready for it."

The ever floating dust that is always present in barns settled on his Sunday, Five-ex quality hat, becoming visible on the surface of it as Jack held it. Wiping his forehead with the other, he thought about their recent harvest. The yield for the season on their wheat had not been great. He preferred to use an older variety of seed for their small, family acreage because it was not so subject to strict patent requirements and all the associated hassle. Jack considered a change. Sometimes he sold some wheat off their land and sometimes holding it in bins waiting for the best price per bushel. Some years Two-Jay just grew milo for silage. Soybeans would also be a good enough crop to make a little money and yet restore health to the soil. They were not in debt and he prioritized the soil, preferring to no-till his crops whenever he thought best.

The cattle were doing well. Mostly Angus, he raised beef for multiple reasons. Money was one of them. The Chicago Mercantile Exchange, or CME in Chicago Illinois, was the ultimate word on commodity prices for beef. A large herd of beef sold by anyone in the area for consumption, would largely have the price per pound determined there. Though selling to one another for stock or trade was common too at varying prices. He had even considered a trade of some cattle for an implement owned by an old friend who had a farm one-hundred-eighty miles to the northwest. As with most things, deals are made day by day.

Stepping back into the post-harvest sunlight, it was still warm. Jack blew the dust off his tan, wool Stetson style hat with a silver buckled leather band around it, and headed toward the house. Halfway there, he began musing about some of the positive sides to marriage. Smiling a deep, wide smile, he looked around instinctively, as if anyone might know what he was thinking. "There would be some definite positives to being married to a fine girl," he said out loud in a normal tone. There were times when he wished for domestic country bliss, as he called it.

"But bliss requires hips! At least some of the time," he said quietly, as he walked in the door of their home. The last thing he wanted to do was encourage his sister in steamrolling him into a marriage with one of her friends. Most of her friends weren't as capable as Julie. He had gotten used to her level of help.

Entering the door he saw her on the leather couch, sewing up a split in a piece of canvas they occasionally used around the farm. The majority of it was spread wide, taking up most of the floor.

"Sunday sis, don't you want to take a break?"

"In a minute. How did you like her?" He knew it. She couldn't leave it alone. He took a breath and held it.

"Julie, I called the pastor and he's available. I ordered new furniture for the house. She's picking up the dress and I imagine a year from now I'll have a fine son in the house. How does all that sound?" When she didn't come out of her silence, freezing him for making joke of it, he tried another approach.

"Honestly Julie, I'm not some pumpkin roller that you have to lead to water. I just haven't found the person yet."

Juliana sat silent. He walked by her end of the deep, leather couch and stopped momentarily to watch her easy talent with an industrial needle and waxed thread. The seams matched evenly and quickly. "You really have the touch!" he remarked, as he brushed her hair gently while walking by her. "You'll really be a great wife yourself someday." Seconds after the comment and turning the corner into the kitchen, he heard her call.

"See! You gave me a good compliment, and you touched my hair. You don't ever do that. You can be a husband and a good one! Besides, I'd like a nice little niece to play with."

"Aha! That's it! he called back. You want a child to play with and you're using our home as the stud farm! Bad sister! For that you can make dinner tonight."

"Already done and in the fridge," she said.

J J

23

At ten-o-clock Tuesday morning the tires on the farm dually saw their last miles. When visiting the Tire and Gun Shop on the east end of Redlands, a person could literally buy either. He walked in and gave the tire size to Nelson who was an eternal compliment to the place. Nelson constituted another of the number residents in Redlands who had submitted years of their life to the Redlands school system sometime in the past. Except in his case, he was about five years younger than Jack and two years less than Juliana. The farm truck was next on the rack in the tire shop as he stepped into the gun room and examined a lever action rifle trimmed in gold and chambered in 44-40. Inside the display case, the rifle was a historical reproduction and although it was designed to function, its real purpose was as a show piece.

"Want to see that Jack?" came a voice behind him. He turned to see Lindsey Wagner. She was still the most attractive unmarried woman in town that he knew of, and the owner of the firearm side of the Tire and Gun Store. Having known her and others around town since they were kids, he smiled. Watching her return one, he saw it as being warm and rich. Now that is something a man want's! He thought to himself.

"No thanks, Linn... it is nice though. Tell you what, I *will* have a bag of that hard candy. No, make that two bags. I might as well make up with Julie. She's been riding herd on me for months about different things."

24

"Still not ready to get married huh, Jack?" She smiled again. This man before her was tall, kind and smart. Any woman in town who had never been down the aisle or many of those who had, would take the opportunity to marry him. In a heartbeat, if the opportunity ever presented itself.

"Now *you've* been talking to Julie! Not fair Linn," he smiled. The red and white check of the gingham dress she wore, though pretty on her did not seem to fit working at either the gun counter or the tire counter, but that was Lindsey. With her soft blonde hair and green eyes combined with light skin, she could make a junk yard look good.

"Oh, just a little Jack," she said, handing him the two bags of candy for free. It was partly to be nice, and partly as a down payment on him. She wasn't shy about things like that. "It's on the house Jack!" He leaned across the counter to kiss her on the cheek and compliment her. "Linn, you are the best part of this store. How come you and I never got together?" he kidded.

"Wasn't my fault," she shot back immediately. "I was even willing to help Julie with whatever if she'd set me up with you, but..." Her sentence was never finished.

"Thanks for the candy Linn, I'll love you the rest of the day!" Handsome, he smiled in a warming, boy-like way as the bell on the door rang when he opened it to leave. "If I decide to get married I'll put a note on your board so you'll have first shot, okay?" She was just able to get a shout out to him before the door shut behind him. "Promises! Promises! "

Mickey

The truck would be ready in an hour. He'd pick it up then, and unload too much money for the tires when he did. He walked the mile out of town to the north grain elevator, near the CO-OP, slipping another of the assorted candies in his mouth every few minutes. He had eaten half of one bag already.

"Might as well give the other bag to the butt pain," he said absently, walking across the yard of the elevator to the office. As he shoved the full bag of candy into his back pocket, Jack looked into the window of the office and turned the handle, pausing at the door. He didn't recognize the beautiful woman at the main office desk, but he knew one thing. It sure wasn't Millie, the sister of the elevator owner. Who, by no coincidence, owned another company who sold to the CO-OP. Millie had been there since before he was able to pee by himself. This definitely wasn't her.

"Hello, you don't look like Millie. Are you?" Jack said, walking through the door.

The woman, probably in her late twenties he judged, smiled back a heart melting grin. In coloring, she looked a lot like Juliana. Brown hair, brown eyes, tanned skin and a confident way about her. She was thinner than Julie, and prettier by far than any girl in the area, even Lindsey. He had never seen her. She tapped the small sign in front of her with a pen, which designated her name as Mickey Hensley.

"Unless they changed that sign, since I can't see the front of it, that's me."

He gave his best grin while sucking down the last of the hard candy. Standing six feet, with tan complexion and a light shade of brown hair, almost a sand color under his cowboy hat; his facial attractiveness was matched by his leanness and strength. The woven belt around his waist with a silver buckle and silver tab at the loose end of the belt finished off the casual cowboy personae, which he lived to the real. The belt curled outward at the point where it exited the last belt loop of the jeans.

"Miss Mickey Hensley?" he questioned. It was obvious that he had looked at her left hand and was interested in her, at least in a curious way.

"Michaela, if you prefer. You have any more of those lemon drops? They make me kind of hungry."

He looked at the bag in his hand. There was one lemon left and a few other candies with it.

"Tell you what! I'll give you this brand new bag of candy," he

27

paused, pulling it out of his back pocket and opening it to look inside. "Containing seven lemon drops and some cinnamon too, if you can give me a duplicate copy of my receipt for eight thousand bushels a few weeks ago. Gentner is the name on it; the Gee is pronounced like the letter Jay. It's for Two-Jay Ranch."

She looked at him as she reached across the desk counter for the bag.

"Okay," she offered back. But she said it with a smile.

Mickey looked around her desk and moved to the computer on it. Within a minute she had printed the receipt and handed it to him. "There you are, Mr. Gentner."

He gave her his best grin again. "Jack please, and thank you Mickey."

"No problem Jack. Stop in again."

He walked the ten feet to the office door, and turning around, smiled one more time, trying to make it genuine. Over his lifetime, he had gotten a lot of mileage out of his smile. From mothers to daughters as well as other odd females here and there. To his credit however, he felt vanity unbecoming for any decent person. Still, that didn't mean a fella' couldn't tease a little.

"Michaela..." he offered, hoping to make a friendship connection. "I like that. I'll come in tomorrow and ask you if you would like to go to dinner at the steakhouse. To save time, you can think of what your answer will be." Her expression changed slightly to one of wry intrigue. It included her eyes. She watched him; assimilating his easy going way and casual frankness.

"Yeah, you be sure and do that!"

Closing the door, he skipped down the steps and across the elevator yard to the street, moving in the direction of the Tire Shop and Gun Store. He would be crossing her view from the window in her office. As he felt her eyes on him, he was sure she would watch him from her seat at the desk.

He shook his head as he walked. "Now *that* is more like it!"

For the last weeks, the weather had been nearly all sunshine and few clouds, but the following day became overcast and heavily so. The smell of rain hovering, the first noticeably cool air of an early fall could be sensed. But Jack walked like a man with a purpose. He unhitched the reins, removed the bit and bridle and removed the saddle and gear from Reacher. With a pat on the backside, he gave him his freedom from the bondage of being a work horse.

A shower, a short ride in the truck and he would be at the elevator. Mickey... Michaela... Mickey... Michaela. He thought out the two names he knew for the woman in the office. He couldn't decide which he liked better, but he knew he liked her. It had been nearly eight years since he had felt the excitement of pursuit. This was just the beginning of course, but it was going to *be* a pursuit, no doubt about it.

By the time he arrived at the elevator, it was raining steady, not hard, just light and steady. Stopping short of the door of the office, he looked at her through the glass. Clearly she was busy, but also well organized and efficient. In his eyes, she was special. Not yet experiencing all of what it was that made her so, she *was* different. Watching her for a minute from the window on the porch, the light rain pelted his long sleeve shirt and wide brimmed riding hat, soaking in where it could. An aged farmer with wrinkles throughout, came up behind him and tapped him on the shoulder, looking at Jack as if he were ill. Mickey looked up as the man entered and shed rain onto the office floor with his arrival. Jack stood just outside staring inward. In a moment she knew. She gave Jack a short smile, looking up at him kindly, in an effort to keep from adding to his unexpected embarrassment. The farmer nodded as she spoke inaudibly to him. She'd seen Jack and his interest of her from outside the glass. Quick glances, looking at Jack through the spotted window, her gaze eventually fell to her desk. She looked pleased. She understood fully. Jack had been admiring her. There was no other explanation. She glowed.

Finishing his business, the man headed toward him. Jack opened the door, still standing where he stood before, in the rain. Allowing room for the man to step out of the office, the elder gentleman, experienced in life as well as farming looked Jack over for the second time. Offering a polite greeting, Jack moved back further to allow him to pass. Turning slightly and looking back into the office momentarily at the girl, the man left the step and went about his business, shaking his head as he left. At this Mickey could hold her humor no more and laughed as a woman laughs when she wants to laugh openly, out loud, but she has to keep it under control. She simply kept her lips together and chuckled out a smile. Her cheeks shined a rose color. Still, she glowed.

"Hi there!" she spoke confidently, alert of his obvious interest.

"Hi Mickey, I wondered if you wouldn't like to go to dinner tonight, at the Cattleman Steakhouse."

Eyeing him, she knew she could work the situation. "You're wet! What were you doing out there?" It wouldn't hurt to tease him, at least a little. He wouldn't be put down this easy.

"Uh, on the first one, it's raining; and on the second, I told you Michaela, that I would come and ask you to dinner."

He sounded casual, and included the smile.

"You told me to think about it," she corrected him. "I've thought about it."

"And?"

"Why do you want to take me to dinner, Jack?"

This was not moving in the right direction. Now she was toying with him. It wasn't a question he had been prepared for, after all; she knew he was interested in her.

"I told you I would come back and ask you out today, and I always keep my word," he said, leaning on the counter now nervous, the smile more forced. For the first time in as long as he could remember, he was nervous with a woman. It quickly became unfamiliar territory.

"So...." she replied slowly. "It's something that you really wanted to do yesterday, but today it's something you have to keep your word on, huh?"

He could see where this was going. He would have to try something different. He put on his best game and took a breath. "Would you like to get married, have a family and live a long happy life with a handsome man?"

This, his charm, combined with his handsome appearance and personality must carry the day. She smiled.

"Oh, I'd like that a lot! Are there any handsome men in town?"

He took off his Stetson and ran a hand down his face. She was loving it! They had barely met, but she already had him right where she wanted him. He was usually so good at dealing with women! He smiled his best smile, accepting that she had him under the gun, and tried once more. "I guess not... but I'd be glad to take you to dinner anyway."

"Oh, you mean it's not a major problem to take me out? I don't eat a lot you know."

Still smiling, he closed his eyes and said one word. "Ouch!" It was a surrender on this round. She had won, that is all she had wanted. She smiled a sweet, embracing smile at him. "I'd be happy to go with you Jack. What time would you like?"

Recovered, he was himself again; he thought. "As soon as your smile is available; I mean, you're available." Cowboy crash and burn! He bent down. His head moved below the counter, pushing his ranch hat up above his head. At this, she burst out laughing in a loud, full heart laugh. "Oh Jack, do you want to go out and come in again and try the whole thing over? I'll pretend it's the first time you came in today?"

He stood in front of her desk shaking his head looking down smiling. The action seemed exaggerated from the turning of the hat brim. Sheepish now, he spoke at last. "I'll be fine if you'll go to the Steakhouse with me when you get off work." She sat up close to her desk and hunched up her shoulders, leaning forward toward him. "Okay, is now alright? I was just about ready to leave. "

"Sounds fine! I don't know what I would have done if you had said no."

"Just watch your step cowboy, and maybe I won't."

J J

Dinner at the restaurant was what one would expect deep in beef country on a Saturday evening in Redlands. Except that it still rained. And its ill effects had fit Jack's earlier efforts to charm her. The atmosphere inside the steakhouse was more optimistic. Always busy, serving mainly steak and potatoes with sides, it became the dinner of choice for townspeople compared to driving forty to one-hundred miles for the same dinner elsewhere. In the evenings at the steakhouse, the feeling is given to small dinner tables which, if not intimate, at least were fitting for small talk. Jack and Michaela sat down along one of the wooden bannisters leading to a second floor, conversing and getting to know one another. Their thin waitress, with a short, bowl cut look to her blonde hair, clearly intended on getting a good tip. After the meal, she made light talk with them as she offered dessert.

"Everything alright tonight?"

"Just great!" Jack replied, not even considering the question. The steak had been at best, mediocre compared to what was usually served. And the salad had been a bit warm, but he didn't care. Being there with Mickey Hensley more than made up for it. Completely unlike any woman he had known anywhere, he cared about nothing else at the moment. When the waitress lingered for longer than usual, Mickey looked up at her. The hometown girl spoke again, looking Mickey in the eye while holding a pot of coffee in one hand.

"You are so lucky, honey! Jack here, is the best man around

town who's still available." She moved the coffee pot she held in unison with her words, swirling it around excessively. Mickey watched it carefully. She could almost feel the burning when the hot liquid would fly out and hit her. The skinny waitress continued to Jack's growing irritation.

"Jack here, is the kind of man..." she said, looking at him up and down hungrily. "The kind of man that every woman wants, even if she doesn't want that kind of man! He's handsome, smart, strong; and even compassionate. Last year I saw him help an old, lame dog that had been around here forever. He took it to the vet and got her leg fixed. Even the dog would never leave him alone after that. No other man in town would have done that! And..." She said, looking up at the dirty ceiling, considering her words. "I'm sure that was a girl dog too!" She giggled an irritating kind of horse laugh that made Jack look out the window at the rain in embarrassment. Once again the rain was a comfort. As she continued, he put his face in his hand. He'd heard enough.

"Look Jenny," he began, but was cut off by the continuing adoration of the woman.

"Honey, he is honest as the day is long, too! Sherry, another waitress, gave him two dollars too much in change once. And don't you know he turned around and gave it right back." She shook her head at Jack in wishful thought. Jack began again.

"Look, Jenny, I'll give you the best tip you've had all week, if you'll just go away and shut up!" At that Mickey raised her napkin to her face and hid her smile. Barely deterred, the waitress left, looking back at Jack while walking to another table.

"I think you have a fan there, Mr. Gentner! That was quite a testimonial!" He looked at his date, sighed in disbelief and then laughed to himself. He could only shake his head, at a loss for words. After a few moments, he spoke. "Oh, Jenny's alright, I guess... but she walks around with too many loose screws you know? Kind of rattles a lot." Mickey broke out in an open laugh this time as he sat contemplating his situation. Still looking red faced, Jack gazed across the room at Jenny. Embarrassed from the waitress's compliments, he was certainly more uncomfortable now than he had been. Seeing his humility as well as his humiliation, Mickey wanted to help him regain his lightheartedness. He being, after all a gentleman, even a cowboy gentleman, he deserved whatever benefit she could afford.

"I'm having a nice time, Jack," Mickey offered. When he smiled, she could see that it helped, but he was still bothered. He responded, wondering whether he should say anything about the exchange or not.

"I didn't put her up to that! You know that, right?" Jack said still frustrated, taking a sip of water in an agitated movement. Mickey smiled playfully, opening her hands wide, one containing a napkin. He looked at her. In more than the obvious way, there was an undefinable something about her that he hadn't figured out yet, making her beautiful.

"How would I know that?" she said, now really enjoying the

evening as she had in her office when he'd sought her out. "She's obviously crazy about you. That's a good thing where I come from."

"She's crazy, I agree with that part!" he smiled. "Talks too much too!" Then, suddenly she saw that he'd lost part of his smile at the situation when he looked again at the thin waitress across the room. He confided in his new friend and most important female interest.

"It's tough for her, you know? She had a guy a few years ago who came into town and he gets her pregnant, then just leaves. Her brother spent a year looking for the guy. Now she has the boy and a tough job working here. She's not that old either, graduated a few years ahead of me. There are others besides myself that try to tip her well because we've all known her forever. And she's a nice person."

It was obvious that this man in front of her was genuinely considerate, even compassionate at remembering the waitress from her youth.

"Is that the compassionate side of you coming out?" she asked, sincerely. He immediately rejected the notion with a head shake. "A lot of people around here are decent people. There are quite a few that will help someone while not drawing attention to themselves. You know how it is."

So this then, was the man who had gotten embarrassed simply asking her to dinner. It was refreshing to meet someone so capable, yet modest. She felt confident about her newfound friendship in him and wanted it to continue as long as possible.

J J

Jack sat on the front porch of their home staring at the rain coming down in that moderate, but long lasting soaking, so common in fall throughout the Midwest. Jack thought intently. Mickey, or Michaela as he preferred, was a different kind of woman. With every other woman he had known it had been no effort to win their admiration. She was like a live and loose bronc, he would have to watch his step every second. As Julie sat next to him, she considered his words as they spoke.

"Well who is she? Where is she from? What's she doing here? What did you both have for dinner?" Julie asked.

"For Pete's sake Julie! Are you with the Sheriff's department? Give me a chance."

"Okay, okay" She waved off his protest," Now go!" she said, undeterred.

They sat on the bench, much as they had when they were kids and watched the rain. It still came down steady after eighteen hours. The sky still heavy and the rain would still come, remaining in the area for the rest of the week.

"Okay, let's see... Her name is Mickey Hensley. She's from Carson and she took over old Millie's spot in the office at the elevator. Oh, and we had steak and potato."

"Uh-huh." It was the statement of a somewhat caring but nosey sister, not quite satisfied with his answers. There was a pause for a minute as Julie digested the answers. Jack just wished for silence so he could stare at the rain and think. That had always been something he had enjoyed the most.

"We know a few of the Hensley families down in Carson. "She said, contemplating it. Then, getting a playful tone in her voice, she jabbed him.

"So... is she hot, Jack?" He sighed; it was obvious, she would never leave him alone until there were five nieces and nephews for her around the house. He was getting irritated; again. Drawing a deep breath before speaking, he gave her the rundown.

"About like you, I guess. She's smart like you, uh... intelligent, um... as tall as you...she's got a nice figure, and a butt like yours." He jabbed back, almost angry. "Really Julie, I don't know... seems to like cooking like you do. As to whether she can handle a horse, I'm not sure yet. Okay?"

"But can she handle a man?" She was outright snickering now. What was it about sisters? Their whole lives, they seemed bent on torment.

"Keep talking Julie! I'll put soap in your contact solution in the middle of the night. Just keep it up." He stood up from the bench, still staring at the rain a moment longer. Turning to the screen door, he grabbed the handle. She tugged on his arm as he pulled the door open.

"Okay, sorry. I love you Jack."

He frowned at her, reached down and pulled her long pony tail, which always seemed to remain perfectly braided.

"I know." he said. "And if you weren't my sister and were a lot nicer person, I could just marry you and save us both all this trouble. But...we all have problems." She swatted her longsuffering brother's tail as he went in, letting the screen door snap shut on its own. He called back to her from inside the house.

"What was all the shooting I was hearing from Nelson's farm as I was coming back in? Was it coyotes trying to get his sheep?"

"No, I called Elle on that. Palmer got fed-up at the grasshopper infestation, them being everywhere and eating up everything. So he just went out back on the porch and started blasting them off the fence with his shotgun. Helps him calm down." Julie said.

"Oh okay, that makes sense." Jack said.

In contrast with the forecast, the following day had changed and called for gradual ending of the rain. Jack Gentner for one, was glad. That was at least something in which he could take satisfaction. Walking to the farm truck, Jack shook his head staring down at the mud now covering the new tires. They had looked new for two days, that was all. Shrugging, he climbed in and started the engine, idling for a minute as he thought. He then turned out the driveway heading east, to the highway and the next county.

Ride

Three hours later he stood cinching up Reacher and wondering how would it go. How should it go? He rode into town with Reacher, wearing a little better jeans than when working, and a little better shirt. He would meet her this clear day, free of rain, a Saturday late afternoon in early October. There was a hint of chill in the air, but enough sun to counter it. They met at the small town's vet hospital at the end of Iron Street. The cattle pens with the gates and chutes were set up in the veterinary yard for treating cattle and possibly some branding too.

He saw her on horseback. Her mount was nose down to the ground, grabbing at the short grass next to the clinic. From the angle he was approaching her, her well-groomed horse looked to be a fifteen hand American Saddlebred. He hadn't realized that she had her own horse until they had walked through town after their dinner date the previous Saturday. They had made a date for this day, a week later, to ride together. His heart skipped a little as he neared them. From the first moment he saw her at the elevator, he had thought she was pretty through the office window. But sitting atop her own compactly built breed of horse, a fine animal, he was drawn to her in a totally different way. She used a smaller saddle for her competition style of riding. He could tell she had done riding at a serious level. It was the way she sat and communicated with her mount.

"Hi Mickey." he said, taking in her impressive presence on her fine horse.

"Hi Jack," she smiled.

He motioned with his left hand toward the grassland east of the veterinary property and town. It belonged to a family that no longer lived in Redlands but whom he knew well. They wouldn't give a second thought to letting him ride their property. Around here a person rarely asked anyway.

She led her horse in the direction he motioned. As she turned her mount it was clear that Mickey was formally acquainted with equitation, the proper riding and fine showmanship of horse riding. Though he didn't know anyone near Redlands who ever took part in traditional equitation, Jack was aware that in the sport, it is primarily the rider that is judged, not the horse. The rider's performance and control, their attire, form and poise, combined with the cleanliness of the horse was the prime interest. They stepped abreast each other for twenty minutes. They were for most of a mile, silent. The soft hoof falls of the horses on the on the semi-wild field, made for a comforting sound when on a second date. Every few minutes one would make short conversation. She spoke first, in a low but confident tone.

"How long have you had Reacher?"

"Almost four... and you?"

"Missy's a good horse; had her five years. We've really gotten to know each other better during the last two though, since I left my temporary job at an insurance agency in Carson. I've been looking at different options in life and have just taken time to think."

For ten minutes neither said another word. When the ground available to ride abreast of each other narrowed due to a cement culvert which ran in the direction of the nearest road, he slowed. The road lay invisible to them but there stood a tree line beyond. Without saying a word he slowed the pace of Reacher until she and Missy stepped ahead. She had expected it. For a hundred yards he followed her quietly.

Admiring Missy and the fine lines of her breed, he was impressed. He hadn't known anyone before who had owned a American Saddlebred. After a mere moments appreciating the fine horse, it didn't take long to observe her rider. In the saddle in front of him, his gaze naturally rose above Missy's tail to the well-proportioned overall appearance of Mickey when in the saddle. In a normal day on the street, he would never have had as good a chance to share her appearance like this for anywhere near as long. Glad that they had taken this quiet route, he traced her from her boots up the legs to the hips and torso. Instinctively he looked to his side. Julie will shut up, for sure. He smiled to himself. As he drew up next to her after the tree line, he spoke again.

"I didn't know that Carson had such pretty women living there. I'll have to visit Carson more often." It was not merely a tease, but a chance taken.

Not responding to his baiting for a full two minutes, she acted almost as if she hadn't heard him; though he knew she had. She seemed to be concentrating on her ride, practicing it. She kept a straight face, bordering on somber. That is what made her a good competitor, and what made him nervous. He had never known a woman like this before. The few women he had been interested in before hadn't had this type of self-control. He was drawn to it. All the women he had known before had always spoke a blue streak, sometimes about important things, most times not. They hadn't been right for him. He knew that. Mickey was captivating, among other things.

When she finally spoke, as they came into a clearing minutes later, she jabbed him again.

"Does that kind of talk work on the women around here Jack?"

He had stepped in it again. The only thing that came to mind wasn't much.

45

"It would, except there aren't any women here on whom I would use it."

"I see," she said.

A quarter hour was spent in silence at the slow pace. She, enjoying her position of temporary control in this new friendship, he, mentally berating himself for such an embarrassing move. He had to be patient with himself though. Most of the women around Redlands wouldn't have even noticed *what* he'd said. But rather that he'd said something. But both Michaela and he enjoyed the ride together. Riding effortlessly, she led him by a half-length. Finally making the decision, he spoke again, and gave more thought to it.

"Mickey... uh... Michaela?"

She drew Missy to a stand. He drew up alongside, his gaze slightly downward and ahead.

"Yes Jack?" she stroked Missy lightly at the mane, examining the braid of it.

"I uh..." he was careful, clearing his throat and picking his words. "There haven't been any women around here that I have been interested in for years. Most of them I just talk to like they are fellas'. If you will come to the house tomorrow afternoon, I'll show you the ranch, let you meet my sister, and in the process..." He paused. "I'll try not to say anything stupid."

Her hat rotated slightly as she turned her head away from him

46

just enough so he couldn't see her face. Smiling, she had him again, and to herself. Seconds passed until she spoke.

"Okay Jack," she said looking him in the eye and with a smile again, this time for him to enjoy.

He hardly knew her, but she captivated him. They both knew that.

"Thanks... uh.. Thank you," he almost whispered. "I ... enjoy your presence."

She waited again, silent atop Missy. An increasing breeze blew the loose hair at the sides of her face, that weren't part of her neatly tucked, French braid.

"I enjoy yours too, Jack." And with a deep, wide, wry grin, she topped it off. "In fact, the less you speak Jack, the more I enjoy your presence." Her cheeks were flush with color at the jibe. It was the color that reflected through the gaze and the cheeks, when a man has begun to win a woman's favor. She brought Missy around neatly, having made the distance out from town at a walk, and after nearly an hour of riding together, she urged Missy into a proper trot as she followed their path back to town.

With Jack following for the full distance, neither said another word. It had been a perfect evening... almost.

J J

"This part is small, just eighty acres, but this along with the two sections we own are all ours. Julie and I run it ourselves mostly, with the help of a few seasonal people. "

"I like it. The beef, the few sheep and you've got a few good horses."

After sunset, Julie had voluntarily stayed to clean up after the three of them shared dinner together. Outside, the fall insects, those still active in the face of the coming month's cooler temperatures, put on their nightly chorus song, the song of the range. The half-moon hung high over the low hills at the east end of their property. With slow steps, they walked around the grounds of the near part of ranch, Jack occasionally making small gestures with an arm in the direction of and about areas of the property.

"We have all new lighting in the big barn and it is really bright. You can even work on tractors or anything else without spots. "

"Pretty nice, Jack." She admired him as he spoke, quietly respecting what he and Julie had accomplished since they had lost both their parents.

They stood in the weak moonlight, a trail of stars above them, beautiful; but not as visible as on a moonless night. Leaning on one of the panels of the current configuration of steel corral, it was cold to the touch. It reminded him to speak warmly to her.

"Oh Jack!" she said, distracted from listening to him. "You've got a big streak of something on your nice shirt. I always hate that! We work hard to dress decent and some little thing..." She rubbed lightly on his shoulder to lessen the spot's visibility.

"Yeah, you're right, he paused, turning to her. "Thank you."

"Michaela, there isn't much else to show you... not here anyway."

"You like using my full name?"

"I do, if it doesn't bother you."

"Not at all. Though, I think you are the only one I know who does."

Quiet for a full minute before he spoke again in the peaceful surroundings and the contented evening together, he looked up. Looking to the sky, he spoke. "Good! I'm glad I am. "

Turning to him, there was enough light to make out a facial expression, but not so much as to see detail. "What did you mean that this was all there was to see... here?" He looked down into the blackening night, the ground barely visible. The single light on the far end of the house property cast little on corral area. It was the only light alongside the moon and stars. He wished he hadn't said anything. Not knowing how to respond, he waited. A few minutes went by. There was no tension, just a soft interest in her voice.

"Jack...?"

"Michaela, there's more to see.... a lot more. Oh, there is... like

I said, two more sections to show you. But..." He took a small breath and exhaled. She waited patiently. She waited two full minutes, knowing that he was now the more silent partner, reversing their arrangement from Saturday.

"Jack? You alright?"

"Yeah. I mean, Yes, I'm okay.

Opening her words in mid-sentence, she continued. Her question hadn't been resolved.

"More to see Jack?"

He would take a chance. He would open his heart; a little. "Michaela," he said, beginning slowly. "There's a lot more to see.

But not here."

"You said that. You have more property somewhere else?"

"No. No, there's a lot more to see, but it's in here." He touched his chest. Continuing in a low and quiet tone, he explained.

"These night sounds Michaela; you would never think during the day that they can be so pleasant at night. You would never know during the heat of day and the business and everything, that they... calm the spirit. They help you think. The wind, the tallgrass moving, the crickets and everything else..." He fell silent, matching the softening night sounds. A minute later, finding the words, Jack gave it up, what he was really thinking.

50

"There's a lot in my heart, inside. A lot that I've saved up for... you know, the right person, the right woman. A guy doesn't want to give his best to someone who will throw his thoughts and feelings in the closet and leave it there for weeks. I know we've only known each other less than a month, but... well, there's a lot inside that I can share as... trust develops. Things that are like the night sounds, you know; deeper friendship. That is, if you would like that Michaela."

She listened to the night sounds more closely than she ever had. They called and replied, sang and spoke. There was an organized concert to it. Leaning her head over on his shoulder, the two stood silent at the cold steel of the corral. It told him that she understood. She'd heard what he said, and what he didn't say. He hadn't proposed or anything, hadn't offered anything dramatic. He just offered to show her the things that he never had offered anyone else. He took her hand in his as the full of night fell over the brush surrounding Two-Jay. Only fifty feet away but seeming much further, a deep and strong horse snorted.

"Pretty sure that's Reach," he said whispering. He gazed across the dark ranch, and kicked the bottom of the corral more by feel than sight in the soft night.

"Michaela, will you do me something, a favor?" Waiting, he searched again for the right words. Usually he was smooth with words, but this was different. "Will you, at least for now, not see other men? He immediately followed the vulnerable request by justifying it.

"I mean, Mich... it's just that there is more present in you, a greater depth and breadth in you... like these night sounds, than in all else Julie and I have out here! There is more in you than in everything we've seen here today. I saw that on our ride, and before. And I'd like to not have to worry that some other man is going to come along and scoop you like the last bag of seed on the shelf." He sighed, that wasn't the way he had wanted it to sound. He was reasonably smart, capable in ranching and farming and able to do many things, and even got the award twice for best Farm and Ranch in the county. But the last few days! He was tanking!

"Oh, Jack, that was a really nice thing to say. I won't. I won't see any other men. At least until we know where you and I are going, right?"

"Right," he said with a little relief and a smile. It was his best, award winning smile for her in the evening darkness. What little moon there was now lay behind a passing cloud. It made the darkness deep enough now that she couldn't have seen his smile if she had known about it. But she felt it.

They moved away from the corral. Tugging her hand gently, he led her back toward the house. Halfway across the distance, he stopped and put an arm around her. She responded with her arm around the middle of his back. She felt the coarse, woven belt around his waist. His silver belt buckle too, easily felt against her stomach as he turned her to face him. Though there

52

was not much more light here in the yard of the house than by the corral, he offered a slow, steady kiss. It was all he could offer her now, but on that he made good. She returned it with softness and a willing heart that is more felt than seen. Walking slowly the the distance to the front door of the house, she listened to the quiet night. It seemed like the first time she'd ever really heard it. He held her hand and with a quiet step up, he grasped the door handle moving back while pushing lightly so she could enter first. He felt her hand touch his middle as a gesture of thanks.

Entering, they heard Julie call from the dining area.

"I have some things to drink here if you are thirsty, you two."

Mickey stopped halfway across the doorway, leaning on the jamb. She touched him lovingly with both hands on his chest and looked up at him in the light of the room. At first she smiled, then began laughing hard enough that she couldn't hold his gaze. She leaned into his chest closing her eyes and laughing in small hiccups of restrained humor.

"Jack ... the last bag of seed on the shelf?" He laughed with her... a little. It had been another *almost* perfect evening. He hung his hat on the wall hanger as Mickey made her way by invitation to the kitchen to talk with Julie. Only minutes later came the echo and eruption of female cackling and hearty laughter of the type that could only mean one thing. A man, a very poor, pitiable man, was being roasted alive. He knew that man well.

Work

Getting a jump on fall work, Jack sat just outside the barn. Above him mostly cloudy skies covered the horizon, with only small breaks allowing sunlight to pierce through. With five boxes of triangular tooth cutting blades at his feet, he replaced the blades in couples on his wheat header. Part of regular maintenance for the machinery that made cutting of wheat possible, it remained at least an annual maintenance chore.

"A box of this and a box of that and soon you're over ten-grand." He voiced to himself, fascinated at the eternal cost of things. Concentrating on fitting the blades together with the screws, he didn't hear Julie slide up behind him.

"Is there enough oil on those?" she said.

"Oh, hi. I wiped them down, if you will give me time. Or do you want to do it?" he suggested.

"Not particularly. I think you are the only person I know that does that. But I finished welding up those broken panels for the corral. Those welding rods you picked up are a lot better for this kind of steel."

Able to do most anything on a farm or ranch, Julie was as good as Jack on most things, better on some. A great welder, a fine cook, and kind of pretty, even for a sister. She sat beside him and put the blades right side up and together for him in an order so could install them quicker. It cut the time needed by half.

"I'm going into town tonight," she said. She watched him as he installed the blades. Want to come?"

Jack looked puzzled. She almost never went into town alone in the evening. Occasionally she would go have a steak, but that was almost always with someone.

"Wasn't really thinking about it. You going by yourself?"

"I am tonight, why?"

"I don't know, just seemed a little odd. Anything wrong?" Jack asked.

"Not really, just felt like getting away for a few hours. By the way, I got to talking with Mickey the other night." Jack corrected her. "Michaela, if you don't mind."

"Hmm. When did you start getting so formal?"

"With her, always," he said.

"You really like her don't you?"

He looked upward and out into the yard, silent for seconds. He watched a cat playing with a mouse during the last seconds of its life. Julie placed the last blades together the way they would need to be installed on the bar.

"Here, she said matter-of-factly." He didn't reach for them.

"Yeah Julie. I do... I really do. I love her. I want her more than anything I've ever wanted. But, we haven't known each other long and ... oh, I don't know."

"Look Jack, you're okay, I mean you're a brother and a man, but there really isn't anything you can do about that." She hoped to lift him a little. He needed it.

"Oh thanks! I can't tell you how much your help doesn't help."

"Okay seriously, just be yourself, and if you care for her, love her! Love her with whatever you have in there inside, you know? Just try to be good at it, huh?"

"What do you mean?" he asked.

"Oh Jack, really! I mean you are excellent with animals and farm machinery, You've got the knack for nearly everything. You even got a patent on your local Ag. Proposal. On top of that you really are handsome. Half the women, no, *any* woman in town would give anything to land you. And, by-the-way buddy-boy, if you ever mention to anyone that I said that, I'll bust you in the nuts and it'll hurt! But, what I mean is, just try to be smart where women are concerned. Does that make sense?"

"Like what?" he said, trying at least a little to see where she was going.

"Again, you have a lot to offer, just be more romantic. I know you know how."

"Oh..." Jack replied, not wanting to hear that. "I guess you're right, but it's never been like this before."

"I know. And believe me she knows that. Some of the things you said to her the other night were fine.. But the bag of seed thing; Jack you can do better than that." Julie put her head into her hands and moved it from side to side. Jack's gaze absently traced over his sister's 'in town' clothes while contemplating what she said. She had a point. He tossed a handful of cutting blades into a box that held the used ones. They landed with a solid clink.

"Yeah, I know. But... how did you know about that?"

"Come on big man! Women talk. We covered you up and down! It doesn't take any time at all for women to get to know each other. She and I were really laughing the other night. She likes you Jack. She likes you a lot. Just relax with her."

"Yeah... I just...want her... you know, so badly! I haven't even been for a ride on Reach in a week. I wan... need... her to complete things. Just like; well, just like the right guy will come for you one day and all of a sudden you will mean the entire world to him. He'll be figuring out reasons to be out here all the time, just to be close to you. He'll be wanting to pay me off just to give him the skinny on you!" She was silent for a minute. He looked up to see her wiping her eyes and looking into the fading daylight. He'd said the wrong thing again. Moving back to his own cause, he continued.

"You're right Julie, I know you're right. I'll make it. It's just that... well... if you lumped every woman in this town, no; the whole county, lumped them together I don't think they would come up to equal her. That messes with a guy. You know what I mean?"

"I know," she sniffled. But you just gave yourself the approach." She wiped her eyes as she spoke, handing him the last blade.

"What do you mean?" he said, tightening the last screw in place.

"Tell her what you just said to me, just like that. You do that, and you'll have her. I guarantee it! And... When you do... I'll be happy for you Jack, really I will. I like her too, like a sister, already."

She brushed his hair softly for a few seconds with her fingers before turning away, like she did when they were kids. They hadn't spoken like this in years. She was actually trying to help. It was refreshing.

"I got ya' Julie... thanks "!

"Okay, just no more bag of feed or seed or whatever it was...

oh!" She trailed off toward the truck, zipping her jacket tight around her middle and calling back to him.

"I'll take Reach for a ride tomorrow, you concentrate on important things!"

Admission

No rodeo of your own? Get your girl down to the local rodeo, the State Rodeo or the National Finals Rodeo later in the year. And pick up your tickets today! She'll want to put the bridle on you, ride herd on you, but you can keep her where you want her at your local rodeo. Get your tickets now, on sale near you!

Confident sounding over the radio, the annoying voice at least gave him an idea. His thoughts focusing, Jack made plans to take Mickey to the rodeo. They were always a good time. He would see her in an hour. He could surprise her and they would talk about it. Dust from another pickup began to fall over the hood of his washed truck as he turned onto Harvest Road. He followed it past the end of town to the local Agricultural Office. Buying tickets there instead of ordering them, he picked up new breed information on selected animals, part of his state agricultural proposal. With just time to get home and get cleaned up before he met with her, he hummed.

Parking the truck and completing a shower in less time than it normally took to clean his boots off properly, he was ready to meet her downtown, in fifteen minutes. The short drive to her rented house in Redlands took an additional five. Knocking on her door before she expected him, Jack took a deep breath of crisp, fall air. The day held good things, he hoped.

"Jack! You made it early! As a matter of fact, I am ready early too. Where do you want to go?"

She stood just inside her doorway in new jeans that made her look desirable. Fitting her figure so well, he knew they had been specially chosen for today. A country top, though not fancy, was fitting just as well. It was obvious that she'd planned her day.

"I've got an answer for you, he said. But *you* will have to decide!" Building mystery, he looked at her waiting. "I'm thinking that we could either, go to the city to walk and shop, go over to Maysville to a nice restaurant, or..." He paused to peak her curiosity. "We could go out by ourselves on some nice grassland I have and have a private picnic. It's a pretty warm day for this time of year. Maybe you'd just need a light jacket. Any one of those works for me, unless you have something in mind?"

"Oh no, no Jack, a picnic is great! I have some big blankets for the ground if you need?"

"Got it covered! I just need you."

She stopped her movements momentarily, looking at him smiling; then recovered.

"Let's spend the whole day together alone," she said freely. "No distractions." She rubbed his arm and pulled the door shut.

He took her arm in a brisk walk to the truck. Once there, they spoke about the previous days, when they couldn't see each other and discussed local fall events. An expectancy rose between them. He leaned over and smiled at her. She knew... it was something... he had something cooking.

"What? What is it?" she said.

"I'll give you a Yankee Dime girl, if you can guess what I have for you in the truck here?"

She offered a full smile. "A Yankee Dime huh? I haven't heard anyone use that phrase since I was a little girl about four years old. My Grandpa used to say that to me before he kissed me." Jack stuck his chin out a little, looking like a thinker. "Sounds like a great man."

"I wish I could guess, but ...?" She looked puzzled, thinking.

"So, you give up?"

"Sure Jack, I give up. What do you have for me?"

He reached into his shirt pocket and pulled out the two tickets that he had purchased at the Ag. Office, being an outlet for nearly everything in the county. He'd bought them less than two hours before. He hoped the whole thing wasn't going to be a bust.

"Jack!" she sounded excited at first but paused in a way that sent a short bolt down his back. Mickey picked up the pace and continued. "Sounds like fun! I'm glad you thought of it. It would be a real kick to watch the whole thing from beginning to end. Thank you. I know we'll have a great time."

"Anything wrong?" he said.

"Wrong?" she replied.

"Well, you kind of hesitated for a second."

Well dressed and surprisingly well spoken, Mickey leaned over on his shoulder, looking through the windshield. Her tone got softer. "No Jack... well, it's just that..." she paused again looking up at him. "I guess I should tell you. It's funny anyway, look! "

As she pulled out her small clutch purse, he saw its intricacy. Impressive in detail, it had been embossed with an equitation scene. She hummed as she opened it. He hadn't heard her hum before. He liked it. At least it meant she felt relaxed.

"Here! I got them for you and I. I thought of you too Jack. Isn't it funny? "

In her hand were two more tickets to the rodeo and state competition. He looked them over as he drove while she held them up. He shook his head. "Hmm... great minds think alike,

I guess." He smiled again, catching her eye and holding it.

"I guess!" She gave his leg a short slap. "Does that...." she began," mean I don't get a Yankee Dime?"

He looked over at her as they drove. Heading slowly away from town on the wide, county road, he put the brake on little by little. He came to a stop while looking at her. The engine rumbled low, as he held his boot on the brake of the truck and put an arm around her. He held her by the eyes more than with the arm. Suddenly she looked as if all her guard was down and she was completely willing to be his, for a moment anyway. He gave her a fast, cheek kiss at first, while pulling her toward him. Her lips rose as she arched in an easy way. They fit together. They belonged together. Seconds spent sharing a soft kiss and an embrace; a gentle embrace, not intense or hurried, just gentle. Leaning back to the wheel of the truck, he looked at her again. She still carried a slight tan from summer.

"You look nice Michaela, thank you for looking so nice today. It's really great after never knowing a woman like you." She stopped. "A woman like me? Tell me what that means, Jack." He thought for a minute.

"Refined, I guess...a refined way of seeing things," he said.

"Well, that's a good thing. I'll try to be refined, if that's what you like. It's clear that you are well educated yourself. And you look nice too cowboy." She leaned on his shoulder again while he eased forward and gave the engine fuel.

"Had any time with Missy this week?" he asked her.

She straightened up a little and reached behind her neck, pulling on her very neatly tied pony tail and thinking of her beautiful American Saddlebred.

"Some. I think she misses me in spite of it being fall and everything, when she seems to like to be outside. "

He looked over at her, digesting her words. "But she's okay, right?"

"Oh definitely, feisty as ever."

"Good."

The low sound of the engine at the first turn of the county road heading east, fit their unhurried mood. They weren't worried about time. It was a day that would lend itself to the sharing of thoughts, feelings and the things they didn't know about each other. Off County road, a short series of smaller, farm roads led within minutes to their site. He had worked up a mystery for her. He slowed and made a short turn onto the property, idling slowly over the parallel bars in the ground at the fence line, the cattle gate. It kept any livestock inside the fence without having to maintain a physical, swinging gate.

Climbing the hill first with the truck and then stopping halfway to walk on foot, they arrived at a spot that lay a hundred-fifty feet higher than most of his land. Turning to her with his now familiar easy smile, he drew her into it. "Look!" he said, almost reverently. He drew an arm slowly against the sky. "This is where I come..." He stood silent and continued, gazing outward. "When I want to think, and aren't pressed by anything." They walked as he spoke. He told her of the land and his family history. "I've never shown this area to anyone." Another fifty feet of walking and they arrived at a grassy side of the hill, free of bare ground, rough patches or branches and anything fallen. Pressed down grass but with no worn spots on the hillside showed that he had been here at least once recently.

"I think it will be fine with a jacket today," he said.

"Oh sure, we'll do something to make sure we're warm enough." The thought of her words sent an ironic shiver down his spine. It was a good shiver. It was the kind of shared moment that you hope for in life... you hope it happens repeatedly over a lifetime.

The wind whistled quietly through a few Blackjack Oak, hardwood trees that topped the hill thirty yards away. It became a symbiotic atmosphere, a balanced point in time. One of those times when you know the moment is perfect, just for enjoyment and you have a person you love beside you to share it. The food placed around the edges of the blanket as it lay on the ground; became arranged partly for weight against the light breeze. They spoke about their horses, their work and immediate goals and dreams. They spoke about ranching, cattle and auctions, and about the desire for family and children. Both of them eating little at first, the door had been opened to discuss love, devotion, what and they wanted most in a mate. In a light way... a playful way, the sounds and words were a melting moment of two people of similar experiences, the same views and the same heart.

"So... I dated her for a few months. She was a nice enough person but she had the viewpoint of an inchworm, just couldn't get a big picture."

Michaela breathed a small, quick chuckle at the illustration but understood. "I know, I know, I went out with a guy a few times but all he could talk about was himself."

The clouds moved gently by in a blue sky on their way to nowhere, but added in the meantime to the beauty of the day. The words and thoughts of the two, sharing sandwiches, the blanket, and personal shortcomings mixed with the successes of their lives matched well. Most of their experiences all occurred within in a limited circle of acquaintances. It was the lament of small towns.

"Redlands has always been my home. It's small and incomplete in many ways, but home anyway. Was Carson a lot easier to live in, being what; four times as large?" Jack asked.

"In some ways, yes. But just because there are more people there, it doesn't mean that there are quality men. I mean many of the men there are fine people and get a lot done, but few of them are what you would call front-line husband material, you know?"

They laughed together. It seemed good, the way they met, the humor, the quiet time together and that they could both walk around in the other's deeper thoughts whether they were together or not. They were increasingly able to step in and out of each other, almost at will. It was a new thing for both. They sensed soul similarities and the value they both shared on the simple, but important things in life. She interrupted him in his asking of her a question while they sat on the blanket.

"Excuse me Jack, but I have to answer a rather pressing call of nature, in those trees over there, I suppose. It was his turn to play the tease, an upper hand.

"Oh, don't worry about it filly. I've been around enough stock yards that it won't bother me much."

"Very funny cow-poke! You can be really funny when you try. Can you try putting away good food so we can talk more when I return?" She started up the hill.

"Hmmm... we've been talking fine... it must be something else you have your mind," he said, mocking her while watching her walk higher. She took slow steps up the shallow hill and called back to him behind her. "Oh you just get cuter and cuter! A little more and you can go on a baby food jar!" He laughed out, finally satisfied that they were close to even. Tapping his boots together on the blanket he didn't move to clean, he watched her walk over the low hill to the stand of blackjack oak trees. Jack couldn't resist one last play. "Don't let anything bite you over there! Let me know if you need help. "Undeterred, she kept her pace but snapped back before disappearing.

"Just going to water the flowers, you big strong man. See if you can get the lid on those plastic containers, okay?"

In three minutes she was back. At her return she had changed her tone, becoming even more contemplative. Her openness to discuss personal matters had widened.

"Jack, what makes you love a girl?" she asked sitting down again.

As he considered the question, she stretched out on the blanket, her lean legs encased in denim. While relaxing on one elbow and facing him, he traced her from head to toe in a matter of seconds. He had been so enamored with who she was inside, he hadn't given as much time to her form, which was also fine! She was indeed beautiful. He saw her boots for the first time. Each had a single gold star embossed on them. Within the gold star there was the number ONE. Why hadn't he noticed them before? He filled in their conversation.

"Hmm... Love a girl?" He had to think about that. They had had quiet times, they had laughed, and had teased. They had been persecuted by each other in playful way; but they had never had straight, serious talk about love. He looked at her, with a slight squint in his eye, musing that she had asked the question so plainly.

"Michaela," he paused, reaching from the blanket over the ground for a blade of prairie grass. He broke it off low on the stem with a soft snap and held it, delicately rolling it between two fingers as he answered. "I'd say... a woman that I can talk to; a woman with whom I can at least as needed, reflect her thoughts." He searched himself further as she waited.

"No, forget all that! I'd say a woman who can hide my heart; keep it safe... with her always, and I'd know that she'll carry it safely like it's worth something, you know? She would protect it and not lose it!"

She looked up at her friend as her head touched on the blanket. She laid on her back. It made her brown hair, that which hadn't been captured into the pony tail, spread out.

"That was beautifully said, Jack, really!"

"Well, that's how I feel it. A heart is a valuable thing, and something too... precious to lose, and certainly something too precious to ignore."

"My gosh Jack, you are sensitive! Juliana said you were, and told me that if I waited long enough, I'd see it. But I didn't expect such a moving answer." He waited, watching the tall grass blowing gently around them before responding.

"I guess after all this time Julie does know something about me," he confessed. But I think about those things a lot, I do. I'm good at some things, better at others, but thinking...um meditating, is something I like to do. And," he added wryly. "I just don't always translate the thoughts into the best color on the palette when standing with a beautiful woman in the dark by a corral."

She held a hand up in front of her mouth to keep from laughing out loud. She gazed at him; off white cowboy hat on his head, with a serious thought behind his kind eyes. She sighed and closed hers. He turned toward her, watching her as the wind blew and she relaxed. Her closed eyes and delicate smile told him, what he would have already guessed, knowing her now as he did. The unbroken continuity of the peaceful day had already had its effect. He slowly leaned down on the one elbow, just above her face as her eyes remained closed. He watched her with desire that didn't ask too much, but rather received what emanated peacefully from her. With the grass blade, its field bloom remaining at the top still in his hand, he moved it underneath her chin stroking lightly, as gently as he could. She smiled wider, her eyes still closed.

"Whatcha' doing there Jack?" she asked softly against the wind in the background.

She knew. She knew that her words put into that one question, words that were left so unguarded and openly peaceful, that they were opening a door together. It was a new place. It was a door to a new room in each of their hearts. In his, a permanent room only for her. It was a question that didn't require an answer. He bent down quietly with the wind pushing the few clouds softly over the low hills, and kissed her gently on the lips. Moving away for a few seconds, he returned to kiss her cheek, It was so soft! As soft as she was beautiful. Everything that he found her to be as a person, was truly beautiful, even the kinds of thoughts she had. He smelled the scent of her hair and laid down next to her, facing the sky.

"I was hoping you would kiss me Jack," she barely whispered.

Remaining still, he stared at the sky overhead and listened to her breathing. It was barely present. "That's an admission, but I'll overlook it," he offered back softly.

Her smile remained, and within a few minutes she relaxed over the whole of her body. He knew she was asleep. It was contented sleep; the gentlest sleep he'd ever seen.

♩ ♩

As afternoon began closing to evening, and though it had been a perfect day, the chill in the air had gotten sharper. She buttoned her denim jacket around her as she sat in the truck with him.

"Turn the heater up will you Jack?" she asked.

"Cold?" he returned.

"Outside maybe, but not inside. It was the best day of my life. The only day that even ever came close was when we rode together." She said.

"Yes, it *was* fine!" he said, almost to himself.

Mickey lay on his shoulder during the slow drive back to

the ranch. She had one hand around his arm for warmth, and the other she put in the crease of his leg and body joint. She squeezed his leg lovingly and patted it occasionally, always replacing it where it had been, as high on the leg as it could be without grabbing for him. Still, it had its effect and it was obvious that this was a seating position that worked well for both of them.

"Having a problem down there cowboy?" she asked, playfully.

"No problem that I haven't had since I met you."

"Aww shucks, is poor ole' cowboy stud ready to go into the stall with the young filly?" She kidded him. He felt, but didn't hear her laughing to herself.

"What is this demented thing that you have going just to torture me?" He smiled, trying his best to look pathetic in the dimming light of fall. It didn't work well with his genuine western personality.

"Just trying to be friendly, cowboy. No offense."

He turned the tables on her. "You know how the lioness treats a mature lion when he comes around for love?"

She sat more upright at the question. "For real? No, what does she do, cowboy?"

"She lets him get close and get his face near what he wants..." He said, waiting for effect, "and then she hits the poor guy in the face with a tail that weighs more than a baseball bat, and is almost as hard!"

She sat up in the seat. "Really? Are you serious?"

"Really!" He said, shaking his head. The poor guy never has a chance. He's gets beat up if he doesn't get it, and beat up if he does!" Jack became quiet, contemplating the unappealing fact.

"I didn't know that... that's interesting. There's a lot I have to learn yet in life," she threw back. He moaned under his breath while turning to the window, gazing at the approaching night.

Missy

A week is a week. Busy for both, they had lunch twice, sat on the porch one evening with Julianna and made a date for Saturday. Their best day to be together, it gave time for anticipation. The middle of November air was sharp and clear. They moved around the dusty stables sharing thoughts, side by side. They spoke knowingly and walked slowly, as if the new experience of being together were taking precedence in their lives. During the last five weeks, they had come to know more of each other. They could largely understand each other, each learning to think in new ways.

Making their way to her rented barn where Missy was kept, they appreciated together the fineness of her breed. Leading the American Saddlebred, their steps fell quietly on the soft dirt as the three together entered the wider practice area she kept for the animal. Puffs of dust rose as Missy moved about there in the fall sunlight.

"Amazing!" Jack breathed quietly.

"You like her?" she asked.

"I do Mick- I really do! An amazing animal, I can tell she can hold her own! I know you ride well together. Equitation, right? I know you're involved in equitation, but you have been competitive haven't you." It was a statement, not a question. "Some," she replied, tilting her head to watch Missy's hoofs as she strode around the corral.

"Do okay at it?"

"I won a few years ago... Missy and I did. We won once at Saddle Seat, and once in Dressage. She's not only a fantastic horse, she's my best girlfriend."

Astounded, he stared at her as if the words hadn't quite formed properly in his mind. He turned her to face him with a finger.

"Are you serious?" His normally soft eyes had a friendly intensity to them now. Looking slightly puzzled, she tried to read him, as to why he was so taken by it.

"Yes, it was a tough competition, no poor showmanship that day, but we made it!" Proud of Missy, and their time together, her eyes went to the well-bred competition horse before them. Though fifteen feet away, she was clearly was in touch with her owner.

"I can't believe that! I mean, I've done a little calf roping and what-not, but winning at what you do? I'm ...." He never finished the sentence.

"Well, I'm glad you're pleased Jack. Really I..." He interrupted her. "The boots right? That's why the boots with the gold star and number one?"

She looked down at the ground inside the corral and nodded, curious what he was thinking.

"Yes, I did that as a personal thing between Missy and me. But her more than me. I really enjoyed those wins, but they were really her wins too! She was fantastic on those days."

"Wow..." he breathed softly to himself while watching Missy in front of him. Mickey came on stronger now.

"Jack, what is this? Why are you so amazed?"

He shrugged, "I don't know, it's just great. I... wish I'd been there to cheer for you... silently, that is!" He looked into her soft eyes, completely taken with her. This girl was something! She was so totally different than any woman he had known. Tough, hardworking, intelligent and not least of them, beautiful. He had a thoroughbred in his life. Finally, she broke his contemplation as her stared at her.

"Okay mister, you asked me all up like that. I have a question for you. "

"Huh?" He shook his head clear. "Oh-okay, shoot," he replied, returning to the present but with his gaze still on Missy.

"What's the 'D' for?"

"What?" he asked, tipping his hat back on his head, still watching the horse.

"The Dee in your name; Jackson D. Gentner. What's the Dee for? What does it represent?" She was emphatic, raising her eyebrows and nodding forward for emphasis.

"Oh.... yeah." He didn't complete his reply, instead turning his face toward the dirt road that had brought them there.

Used to giving him time when he was thinking, she finally gave up waiting.

"WELL?" Her tone increasing. He looked back to Missy and then down, kicking the bottom wood rail of the corral. "Just my middle name."

She rolled her eyes. "Okay, SAM SMART! GIVE-IT-UP! "

"Oh, Mick!"

"Give it up, Mister!" She punched him in the chest with her index finger. He paused before answering and sighed.

"Dilbert." he said.

She stood staring at him, trying to determine whether he was on the level, or avoiding answering. Raising her eyebrows again and tilting her head, she made certain of him telling her the truth. She questioned him again, more softly.

"Dilbert?"

"Yep, Dilbert; my Great Grandfather's name. He was a great cattleman around here ages ago."

"Dilbert?" She repeated again in a stronger tone.

"Yup."

"Dilbert!" She now was venturing into laughter, mixed with restrained giggling.

He turned to her and answered sharply, but knew she had his number again. "Yes... Yes... Dilbert, okay?"

Open mouthed and holding back a gut busting laugh, she repeated it again.

"Jackson, Dilbert Gentner?"

Yeah, yeah.... yeah... "He blew out the last word in an exhale, spitting into the corral.

Mickey laughed openly now, bending slightly from the humor while leaning on the top rail of the corral. She closed her eyes hard laughing..

"Dilbert... Dilbert, Dilbert, Dilbert! Aww haw!"

He came on hard. "Look! I'd hate to have to swat your ASS...SET, right here in front of Missy, but I WILL! BELIEVE ME, I WILL! " At that, she laughed harder.

"My Can-Do man! Strong and tough, gorgeous and intelligent, insightful and captivating! Dilbert! "

He had had enough. He grabbed her, still laughing and bent her over his knee next to the corral, pausing to give her a chance. She put a hand over her mouth, but it wasn't enough. She laughed through it. He firmed his lips, took a breath and swatted her butt four times, hard. Too hard, he thought afterward. And he was instantly sorry. Even though he hadn't lost his temper and never would with her, Jack thought he'd been too hard in his play with her. Lifting her, he searched her expression. Though the laughter had diminished, there was a small smile that still remained. The light of affection still shone in her eyes. She wasn't fragile, nor was she hurt inside, she could take it! Pulling her to him, he held her close. She knew he was sorry. He kissed her harder and longer than he ever kissed any woman. She understood. She knew he would never let her go. That was all she wanted.

"Michaela, I love you so much! Lord help me, I love you so much!" He buried his face in her neck while gripping her arms with the hand strength of a rancher.

"I know Cowboy! I feel the same. She slapped his back firmly and loudly; partly in response to the spanking. She responded to him intently, feeling his desire for her. It was obvious that he was hungry for her. Embracing the hunger, they were two people made one by a standing embrace.

Ten minutes, mingled with snickering brought a calm. But things were different, now deeper between them. Missy made her way in slow steps to the edge of the corral where they stood. Her big, dark eyes watching, concerned. Mickey, opening an eye from the embrace, saw Missy move up close. She relaxed her embrace on Jack, but allowed him to still retain his on her as she turned in his arms to face her best female friend in the world.

"Okay girl, it's okay. "I'm just learning *my* routine." The dark, chestnut American Saddlebred seemingly winked in an understanding way and inched away from them. It was another day in their lives together. An important day.

J J

Julie stirred the mashed potatoes with a wooden spoon as the three of them spoke in the kitchen and dinette area. She froze and stared at her brother.

"JACK! You hit her?" Mickey jumped in to save him. The spanking between them, had long since been lovingly consigned to healthy discipline.

"No, no Julie, I got a little out of control about his middle name and he had to um... reign me in."

"I busted her on her best parts, is what I did!" Jack said smiling.

Still open mouthed, Julie looked to Michaela for confirmation of truth, holding the potatoes stretched outward in one arm and the spoon far outward in the other, gesturing... questioning. Mickey had a hand over her mouth as she sat at the table, and with eyebrows raised, nodded to the affirmative. "He burned my assets, as he called it."

"Jack! You really are a clod! It couldn't have been that bad." Julie said. And went back to stirring, angrily now, with a burning, periodic stare at him.

"Nope, I really pushed him to it, Julie."

"Oh, what would mom say back in the day?" She asked out loud, looking out the window of the kitchen shaking her head. Turning, she shook the spoon at Jack. "WHAT WOULD DAD SAY?... hitting a woman you want to.. mar... um.. HITTING A WOMAN! She changed course quickly, and recovered from potentially embarrassing herself, or all of them. "You really are a ..."

His capable and smart sister concentrated on her cooking but still mumbled a little, her anger adding to her natural, country beauty. Jack came over to her to help with the cooking.

"I can handle this! Get out of the way! And another thing OLDER brother!" She shook the wooden spoon in his face. You better shape up or I'm going to serve you UNCOOKED, COLD TAPIOCA PUDDING, Buddy boy, Got it? "

At this last exchange, Mickey burst out laughing again and looked at Julie, who smiled over at her warmly with dark, but sincere eyes. Jack, working on the statement, didn't understand. He mouthed the word questioningly back to Mickey. He knew he'd been burned by the camaraderie of womanhood, he knew it

82

wasn't good, but didn't understand. After a few minutes of intermittent snickering by them, He looked at Michaela. She explained.

"Tapioca is delicious and good... when cooked. When it's uncooked, it's deadly!"

"Really?" Jack asked, now fascinated. He honestly loved learning new things.

"Oh REAAALLLLY ?" Julie mocked him overtly for being so weak in his cooking skills.

Mickey nodded and began finishing the explanation. Julie interrupted her. The agitated sister polished him off while the sound of the food going into the oven clanged from her frustration at her older brother.

"He's a cooking kindergartener Mick, you may have to use baby talk." He frowned, looking to the woman he now loved more than anything else in life. She finished the explanation, followed by Julie's sharp barb when Mickey had finished.

"Yeah! It's totally toxic when uncooked; Boot Hill Cowboy! So... WATCH IT!" Julie said.

Julie picked up the wooden spoon, still containing bits of the mashed potatoes on the end. She held it under her chin and made a cutting motion, imitating a cut throat. As the end of the spoon came by her mouth she stopped and licked the spoon clean, smiling. He digested the joke and stood to leave the room.

Jack had to defend himself at least a little before being driven away by abuse, however.

"Aww... she's just jealous, because I told her that if I hadn't met you and she wasn't my sister, I'd want her for a wife.... she's so sweeeeeet!" He swatted his sister on her rump with a loud smack as he walked by her. Juliana rolled her eyes and looked briefly out the kitchen window again.

"OH, Lucky Me!" she spoke loudly. Turning, she wrote on her chalkboard grocery list...' T-A-P-I-O-C-A. Mickey laughed, loving the underlying affection between them. That affection was enough to allow dinner to be eaten without further incident or insult as the three connected, reminiscing about family history. It appeared there was a chance that they could all three be a family one day.

Lelo

Jack Gentner surveyed the southernmost three acres of his half section that lay by the river. There were a lot of old tree branches of all sizes, and river flotsam that had been brought high onto land by flooding in the nearby creek the year before. Most of the debris, Jack had gathered into eight to twelve foot piles, wide at the base for disposal by fire. Surveying the area a week before, he decided it was usable, just covered with debris.

As Lelo dismounted his ancient backhoe, he removed his hat and gained a view of what he was portending to do. With short, grey hair and new overalls and English beret cap, his uniqueness was known in the county. His vision not too good, and his hearing almost non-existent; bladder problems and heart issues plaguing him as well, he was the definitely the hardest worker in Grant county.

"Ye' want all them sticks piled up to burn- zat it, Jake?"

Jack smiled, overlooking his mispronounced name.

"Right! PUT THE LAST LOOSE DRIFTWOOD IN A PILE TO BURN! THE OTHERS ARE READY," he yelled, making sure he was understood.

"Ooookeyy... pile n burn... pile n burn." He walked away muttering. "Shure hope I ain't seein' no squatters out heah.' Them state boys don't like it much when ya shoot em." He looked around as he made his way to the old machinery, muttering.

The backhoe, by Jack's calculation, had come off the assembly line some time during the last years of Jack's grandfather's life. As it wheezed and choked out diesel exhaust, it moved as it sounded. Slowly Lelo brought the hulk to bear on some of the wood nearby that lay loose around the field. The debris began to move toward the already existing bonfire piles. Jack watched for a few minutes until he felt that Lelo had the task in hand. Leaving after five minutes, he hurried down the road, late to collect cattle from their dip at the vet.

While paying the fee for the vet service and nearly ready to haul out the ten head of Angus, his phone went off in the truck. It was Macsun, the diesel service man who used his small tank truck for bringing fuel out to remote jobs in the field, like the one with Lelo.

"Jack, Jack! You better get back down here to the river acres, I think something's wrong."

Leaving the trailer temporarily at the vet, he would load

the cattle when he returned. He navigated the old, rutted and holed road in his five year old truck at highway speed, fascinated that something could have gone wrong with such a simple job. Arriving fifteen minutes later, he got out of the truck with an open mouth, but no words. The driftwood and tree branches were loose, and burning everywhere, right where each piece stood. The piles that had been made before, were simply scattered completely over the field, burning in every direction. A hundred small fires burned erratically where there should have been twelve steady ones. Not one organized pile was left whole for burning.

Macsun, a man in his fifties in overalls and a too healthy sense of humor, but otherwise of sound mind and body, came walking up to Jack as he arrived. He spoke like he had a mouthful of rocks; through a wooden match he had in his mouth, like a cigarette."

"Ain't it a mess Jack? That Lelo ain't the man he used to be! The last five years have been pretty rough. Old man Swanson tried ta 'ire him layst ye'ah and Lelo plum run over his whole shed, windows and all... didn't see it! I once seen him mow down a big outhouse the same way! And if he can't see a shed, he ain't gonna' see them piles of sticks! Oh, Lelo said he had to go get his heart medicine, might be back today, might not. The way he was workin' it out there wuz... He'd make one run to pile stuff, and would knock down two others that were already burning at the same time. Burning stuff scattered everywhere! "Ain't it a mess?"

Sick at the sight of it, Jack surveyed the field. He'd spent nearly two weeks piling up the majority of the flotsam that was now all over the field. As Jack mounted the old backhoe, he surveyed the field. He would try to clean the mess as best he could. After putting a small area of the field in order again he had the wood back in piles. He pushed the new gatherings higher while running up them vertically on the dirt base. Raising them for effective burning. Near the moment when he was about to finish a large one, the backhoe blade climbed about twelve feet to the top. At the peak, the steering wheel came off in Jack's hand. There had been no lock nut to hold the steering wheel on the shaft. As he tried to apply the brakes to hold him in place while he reattached the steering wheel, he discovered there were none. No brakes on the machine at all! With no steering wheel and no brakes, he slipped the transmission into neutral and let the creaking pile of junk roll backwards until it stopped near a ditch that lay behind him. Macsun came up again as Jack shut down the motor which sounded unmistakably like a cement mixer.

"Should a told ya' Jack, He ain't had any brakes on that thang for years."

Jack nodded to Macsun. "Won't need you anymore for this job Mac, thanks."

Fences

"Jack?"

Juliana held four large U-shaped fence staples in her mouth while pounding another two home in the fence post in front of her. She was tough, even aggressive when, as in other things, repairing fence. Attractive and intelligent, it made Jack stop to watch her from time-to-time. Her dark hair and modest, but not skinny figure would appeal to some man, one day. Even as a brother, he could see that. There were times when he couldn't figure out his sister. Working their south acreage fence together, she continued.

"What ya' thinkin' bout?" she asked. He smiled. Spitting out a staple, he recounted the story of Lelo and the mess he had created a week before. He had never told her of it. They laughed together. She thought, and then countered him.

"How about that seasonal guy who reached for a shovel by that trough, and was struck at by a rattlesnake that surprised him! He fell back and broke his finger. And I had to come to kill the snake!" Julie said, as Jack shook his head, recalling the day.

"And the one guy who was short a horse! He tried herding cattle on his Harley!" he said, laughing. She leaned heavy on the fence, also releasing a hearty laugh. A person saw strange things in the country. They stood quiet for the better part of a minute, working. Then both tried to speak. Jack got his words in first.

"How about Paul, down there in the bottom, pulling that small disk with a jeep when his tractor went out?"

Julie wailed, recalling it. "And do you remember Charlie, the horse? You know, Charlie-Horse?" she said, then continued. "And How about Five Toes?"

Jack smiled, "Yeah, five-toes that six-toed cat! What happened to him?" She shrugged her shoulders, continuing the banter.

"Oh, and how about that old guy who never could remember the name of 'Bumble' when he called that cow we had; he kept calling her 'Pussy Red!" He was a good worker and Dad liked him a lot but the guy just couldn't control his mouth. I was young and Dad didn't want me hearing that, so he fired the guy."

They stood now swallowing water, really looking each other in the eyes. They hadn't in a while. Shaking her head, she continued.

"Remember the guy who lived down by the river who tried to get his dog used to noise, so he kept throwing firecrackers in the dog run! That poor animal. You never could move quickly around that dog. He ended up neurotic!"

"YEAH! I remember!" Jack said, intently. "I was helping him out once, feeding his stock and I moved too quickly, just one time. He took a bite out of my leg and it took six weeks to heal." Julie spit out some staples, rather than talk through them.

"I remember that! And how about Rogue?" she replied. "Old Rogue Bull went where he wanted; all nineteen-hundred pounds of him! When he wanted a cow, you know, right now; he would walk right through a four wire fence and pull out at least five posts! "

One by one, they countered each other with stories, working only fifteen feet apart as they passed each other repeatedly walking down the fence line. It had been a rich life they had together, and they knew it. They hoped it would never change. They both however, knew it had to... someday, one day.

"Jack, I was a little hard on you about Mickey. I'm sorry. You have a right to do things your way. You do most of the work around here this time of year anyway. "

"Aww Juul, you're fine... and not too bad of a sister when you're not threatening people or killing things. I didn't pay it any mind. But I'll tell you this! If you and our Maker will both help, I'm going to marry her."

Julie pulled five staples from her lips. "You know I'll help Jack.

I love her too, already, I do. And..." she went silent as she pushed the loose wire at the top of the fence back into place before beating the staple into it.

"And what?" he spoke low, distracted by his own part of the fence, working the wire into place before hammering the staples.

"Oh... I think..." Julie faded off to mumbling as she slugged a few more staples into practically the only good wooden post left.

"These old posts! Dad put these in thirty years ago." She said absently. "I think you two will have a great life together! After I get out, that is."

"Out? Out what?" Jack said.

"Out of the house, dummy!"

"Huh? What do you mean?"

Julie stopped hammering and took a break while leaning on the fence and shaking her head at her brother, looking over at him. Brothers and sisters in any age always think differently. She turned to him, still breathing deeply from hammering her personal fears into the fence.

"Jack! Come on Jack... EARTH TO COWBOY JACK! If you two get married one day, even in the far future, I'll have to find some other kind of living space."

He sat on the nail bucket and propped up his boot on the lowest wire of the fence. Reaching behind his neck to scratch with the claw part of the hammer, he considered her words.

"Never even thought about you going anywhere. I mean, I figured you would just stay in the house."

Quiet for only seconds, she then laughed openly, leaning over the railing and turning her head under her dust colored cowboy hat toward him, just staring.

"That's because you aren't a woman, Jack. Do you really want nosey sister around, banging and clanging in the kitchen while you are having fun and games in the house with Michaela, chasing her around without clothes or whatever? Hmmmmmm? "Her voice raised in pitch as she made the long sarcastic remark and accompanying dumb face.

"Oh." he said. At that, Julie spit out a laugh and reached for more staples in the bucket. Jack stood still, his gaze tracing over the land. She hammered for a few minutes while he thought. Finally he spoke.

"Julie, if Mickey and I get married one day; I hope so, and if we do, you will stay on the ranch and if possible in the house. Because I wouldn't have it any other way! I've known Mickey for about two months. And I've had you on my back for twenty eight years! You and I have worked this place together, side-by-side even when the folks were alive. We have time here! We are part of each other in a way no one else could be. I don't think I could get by without you being a pain in the butt. Besides, you're a

93

better welder than I am! Who would do the welding?"

She looked over at her older brother. He loved her. In spite of everything in life, they really loved each other. He stood up and stretched, back to normal in the tick of the second hand on a watch.

"I'm going to the house for lunch. Get in the truck or I'll leave you out here! Oh." he paused. "And don't say a thing or I'll... I don't know, kiss you or hug you or some other kind of self-humiliation." She stood still as her loose hair, usually tied back, lifted and fell in the light breeze. Tossing her hammer into the bucket sitting on the ground, she walked slowly to the pickup and sat in the bed. She loved Jack, and Two-Jay. She wiped her eyes with one hand as she gripped the inside of the truck bed with the other. He started the engine and called out the window before putting it into gear.

"You better hold on, or I'll dump your lousy butt in a ditch!"

Holiday

"Michaela sat on the leather couch, half falling into the depth and breadth of it. Thinking of Missy, she nervously stood now and then, moving through the ranch house to the rear of the main room. Gazing out over the attractive and well organized sections of the grounds around the house, she watched the barn and corral a hundred yards distant. Waiting a minute, she saw Missy stepping her way around the unfamiliar corral, watching and listening, twitching her ears and stretching out her neck slightly when she caught an unfamiliar scent. It was the best idea to keep her here and save the money from the rented stable. She had just thought of Jack when he walked into the room.

"Thanks again Jack, for letting Missy stay here. And me the first night! It will help me feel okay about her out there for tonight and in the long term, it'll save me boat-loads of money."

"No reason not to, we had the room. Besides, it's a good idea to get both she and you used to being around here. You never know when both of you might be stabled here!" She turned to him grinning, and kissed his cheek, her eyes immediately falling again on the fine and expensive equine out the window. He knew Mickey was still a little nervous about leaving her horse here. He distracted her.

"Sugar Cookie?" he asked, offering her one. "Sugar cookies have been a part of Thanksgiving and Christmas here since the place opened, since the eighteen-seventies."

She took the holiday confection, tasting it.

"Mmmm... Good! Thanks... you or Julie?" she asked, holding up the cookie.

"I can make em', but she'll always be better in the kitchen."

It was nearly Thanksgiving. The elevator, almost closed for the week, conveniently aided her schedule with Missy. Likewise, most of the busy work was complete at the ranch except for the daily feeding of the livestock. The commonly experienced clear air of late November, missing this week, gave way to gusty winds and low clouds.

"Maybe the wind is making Missy a little nervous. I'd better put her inside."

Jack ate the last of a cookie and watched Missy across the grounds. "Mmmm hmmm, would be good to..." he said impolitely, as he chewed the cookie at the same time.

She pulled a sweater over her head and stepped out the

back door of the main house, having to pull the door twice against the pressure to get it latched against the wind. The wind blew her loose hair in all directions. When riding or working she always wore a pony tail. In times like this, around holidays or special occasions she tried to appear prettier, more celebratory, leaving it loose or even curling it. Today she had to hold part of it in one hand while she moved across the grounds to the barn. Approaching the skittish horse from the off-side, the side from which a person doesn't mount a horse, and circling around, Mickey observed her. Patting and putting her at ease as the wind increased, a gentle tug was all it took to get the show horse to move across the open corral into a stall in the barn. She immediately showed signs of contentment.

"Silly of me to leave you out there! I was just trying to let you get used to the place for a little while, your new home and all. We'll practice this week, honey. We both need it."

Though Julie had been coming up fast as a friend to her, Michaela couldn't help but love this fine, intelligent animal, her best female friend in the world. They had worked hard together and won. Getting through life's toughest challenges and coming out on top... that's winning!

"We'll try again this next year too. With you, I know we'll make it!

J J

By the fireplace three days before Thanksgiving, the three of them ate the beef and potatoes with salad and Julie's thick, homemade bread. They laughed and ate while Jack and Julie recounted the stories with Mickey that the two had shared while mending fences.

"No television?" Mickey asked, at a pause in the laughter.

Licking his fingers, Jack missed the question from Michaela.

"I said, no TV here? I've never noticed before that you didn't have one." Jack motioned toward Julie as he took another bite and chewed. When he got the bite down, he filled in the blanks.

"Julie has one in her room. I don't really need em'. If I want to watch a little something on a rare occasion, I'll go crash her room for a bit. You know, drag a chair in there, but I basically don't need it. Too much to do around here and," he wobbled his hand like an unstable bird as he ate more of the beef, and stopped short of finishing the sentence.

"Too much love," Julie interjected. Michaela looked at her, then Jack and smiled slyly. As the wind rose and fell in almost roller-coaster type rhythm, Mickey clearly distracted, fought an urge to check on Missy.

"She's all buttoned up," Jack said. "We shut all the doors and she's all cozy!"

Mickey had locked her up personally and knew it, but being the first night, couldn't help wondering. She glanced to Julie who sat on the fireplace hearth, knees together with atypical good posture, wiping her mouth with a napkin. She'd just finished her meal. She was only two years older, but she seemed to be both a sister figure and a mothering type as well. She would make a good sister-in-law and confidant.

Julie comforted her. "We'll go check her before we turn in Mick, she's fine."

"Of course! I know... It's just me. It's just that...well, besides being my partner, she is pretty valuable."

"I know babe." Julie said. "We'll check her."

Julie stood to take in the plates. She stood in front of Jack waiting for his.

"By the way Jack, I put new sheets on the bed for you two." Jack had only half chewed the last bite. He stopped mid-way to swallowing, his mouth open. He stared at his sister. Mickey's eyes became full and tense. Her grip tightened on the armrest. Both he and Mickey looked at Julie and then to each other almost in unison. Each wondered if there was something they didn't know that the other did. Julie was confused at their reactions waiting for the plates until her words sank in.

Julie shook it off, only a little embarrassed. She turned only a little pink and smiled. "I meant for each of you! On your own beds. Of course, we aren't to that place yet, are we?"

Jack wiped his mouth and threw the napkin in the plate as he sat it next to his chair. His eyebrows went up and his jaw muscles tense.

"Well, you sure got from me to we in a hurry! You used to just bug me about finding a wife, now we're all using the same sheets! One more slip like that sweet Juliana, and you will be outside in the cold with Jupiter; your horse or the planet, I don't care which!"

Julie and Mickey looked at each other. It had been funny, but it brought to the surface what they had all been thinking. Mickey gave her a forgiving smile. Julie motioned with her head for Mickey to follow her. They walked into the kitchen laughing.

"You got us pretty good with that," Mickey confessed. comfortable that there was only two years difference between them. Gladly their camaraderie had already filled in some of the missing pieces in their lives.

"I thought Jack was going to crap his pants! Julie laughed, offering a high-five to Mickey, partly to celebrate their rapidly growing soul-sisterhood.

"To be honest, I almost did myself!" Michaela responded quickly. "I thought Jack must have been giving you some delicious manure about how he and I have been getting on with it, and you decided to help the cause!"

Two sisters, of the heart at least, laughed together a rich, heart bonding laugh three days before Thanksgiving.

"You know Mickey, since you have been around here, we have had so much more laughter! It was hard for several years, just he and I, but we made it. And it sure is nice when you're here girl!"

"I think so too," Michaela smiled. "Especially when we see him like that!"

J J

"JACK! JACK! GET IN HERE! GET IN HERE RIGHT NOW!" Julie yelled down the hall of their home. "And don't act like you are asleep... YOU! IN HERE, NOW!"

Within seconds, the thirty-four year old cattleman and Mickey, the joy of his life; both burst into the hallway out of their respective rooms as if from paired places in a starting gate at the Kentucky Derby. Rushing down the hallway, both burst into the kitchen at the end of the short race, just as they begun it, together.

"What's going on? What's the prob'..."

Both of them immediately saw the problem. The sink had backed up and dishwasher pump was running, pumping soap suds from the dishwasher through a line under the counter into the sink forcing it to overflow. The soap that he had bought for the dishwasher as an afterthought earlier in the day, although made for convenience, wasn't a type for automatic dishwashers;

and he would pay for it. He had bought it, literally and figuratively. With soap and water moving across the floor at a faster rate than could be intercepted and soaked up, Julie worked feverishly and angrily. From the sink, over the cabinet and onto the floor flowing in white avalanches was an eternal fresh supply of water. There was however not only the sink to contend with, but water and soap also flowed out of the dishwasher to which it was attached whenever the washer was opened. The livid sister had buckets, a mop and rags. She was using all of them at the same time, rotating from one to another. There was however nowhere for the suds to go. Having in fact been asleep, Jack stood watching the white blizzard. He was still not fully awake when Julie threw an oversize bath towel at him.

"There!" she said, as the soggy towel pasted him in the chest, granting him a full awakening all at once. As it hit him with a splat under the chin, soaking him, it still dripped as it fell to the floor.

"Get over here and help me clean this! This is YOUR FAULT!"

As they worked together to stop the dishwasher and clear the suds inside, the white snow would pour out of it. When they closed the door to run water though it to clear the suds inside the washer it only increased the suds running from the sink. The floor, with half an inch of water on it, became a pond. Mopping wouldn't keep up. The automatic drain pump on the dishwasher kept activating to clear the remaining water in the washer when the door was closed. When it was opened the suds and water were pushed back out the washer side.

"Let's figure this out," Jack said, becoming interested in the cause rather than the result. He looked into the drain and reached into the washer to examine the soap. It wasn't what Julie wanted. Frustrated as only women can be when placed in such a situation, she screamed again.

"STOP IT! STOP IT JACK! Just help me clean it. I don't' care what caused it!

When he wouldn't, Julie soaked up what was running down the front of the cabinet, while Mickey used the mop and dumped the water out the back door. When the second, large bath towel became full, she wrung it out over her brother's head while he lay on the floor, trying to determine the problem. He disregarded it as if it were rain, to Julie's added frustration. An hour after all three had begun working as a defacto-team, enough of the soap had diminished that they could gain ground against the flood.

At a quarter-to-one in the morning, the water was gone and the floor clean. All three were wet with soap and sweat despite the cool air that had blown inside has Mickey had thrown buckets of mop water outside. Julie, who had come into the kitchen before bed merely to run the dishwasher for the morning, stood in only a night tee-shirt and no bra. Standing soaked to the skin and glaring at Jack, squinting. She said nothing else. All three were soaked. Pajamas, night shirts and shorts all soaked, but the tile floor lay clean and sparkling. Each heaved a sigh and sat down on the tile, wetting it again from the dripping clothes.

They sat, eyes closed and heads back, wishing for sleep. After a short breather, Julie stood, and left without another word, snapping off the kitchen light on her way out.

Mickey peeked around the island of a table in the center of the kitchen in the semi-darkness. Quiet until one of them would speak, neither wanted words. Slowly they found each other as she met his seeking eyes. They managed a connecting, weak smile. He moved close to touch her cheek as she took her rest on his shoulder, sitting on the dark kitchen floor.

"On you, wet has a nice feel," Jack said. It had been the only thing said, as he leaned next to her to kiss her cheek. Putting both arms around him she returned the affection on his lips. Sweet kisses repeating rhythmically, were followed by a sigh as Jack stood to help lift her to her feet. Mickey standing, he kissed her again. Subdued desire for her had risen. He carried her to the couch of the den. Laying her on it, he kissed her continually with the lights off throughout the house. Tenderly, he offered gentle kisses as he made his way across her wet clothes. Both of them shared fits of quiet laughter from the ridiculousness of it all. Her pajamas, thick with dampness and soap, provided an unromantic shield against his attention. All of their clothes were flavored with soap. At her knees, he simply laid his forehead on her legs and closed his eyes. All the water and all the soap would clean and dampen his desire, even to kiss her for tonight. Watching Jack moving in shadows across her in the dark room, she ran her fingers through his soap and sweat soaked hair.

"You're handsome, you know? At least, what I can see of you." He moved to lay his cheek against her face.

"I want you Michaela. That's all...just want."

"I know, me too." she admitted her desire.

A light kiss on his forehead to break the tension brought the night to a conclusion.

"You taste like soap," she offered.

"You taste like love," he said.

A watery imprint of the clothes were silhouetted into the fabric of the couch, but unseen in the darkness as they stood. "The hazards of running a ranch!" he said. She kissed him one last time; a very contented kiss on the lips. "Goodnight, Jack"

He leaned over, his arms around her, held her close and kissed the top of their head.

"Goodnight, honey."

Routine

The day before Thanksgiving the temperature held at a chilly forty-five degrees, significant for late November. As Michaela sat atop Missy, she gave simple direction to her mount, walking her through basic rhythms and turns. Some were without aid of course orienting elements. Some of the work the two performed were assisted by simple blocked areas or a portable rail, which could be set to any height. As Missy offered her efforts to provide a steady walk, trot and canter; Michaela practiced her vertical alignment and riding to cause a minimum of distraction for her partner.

Jack and Julie watched Michaela and Missy perform their most basic routine, which they use to warm their minds and make acute their reflexes. Like a strings player who uses various suites by a composer to keep their dexterity in play, they used the routine to tone-up and share time together; to remain fresh. With each graceful move they made, Jack would gain a new admiration for Mickey. She had not only captured his heart, but earned in the truest way, his respect. Julie, familiar with western competition, particularly barrel racing, admired her only distantly as a rider, understanding little of the routine. As a woman however, she understood Mickey fully. They both loved her already.

Wearing her competition clothing that Missy was used to seeing, it brought Missy focus and allowed the lovely equine to ignore the change in surroundings and perform as she should. Smaller than a western saddle, the equitation saddle, whether for Dressage or Saddle Seat work, allowed for the movement required. The twenty minute routine, performed as if she and her mount were the only ones present, ended fluidly. Their exercise complete, Mickey dismounted in the same spot that she had lifted into the saddle as Missy stood in the corral. It gave the horse her first taste of Two-Jay as an exercise arena. Michaela spoke easy and softly to Missy and led her into the barn. In the stall for Missy, Michaela ran a hand down over the beautiful horse's withers whispering her affirmation. Leaning into her, Michaela pressed her head against Missy's neck. It was part of the personal routine for them. Closing her eyes, she heard Missy's heartbeat. She heard her breathing and felt the rhythms of her muscular tightness over her body. It evidenced her post exercise contentment. When she wasn't comfortable a vibration or twitching of her stomach muscles reflected it and could be felt through her upper muscular system. Today she stood relaxed with little agitation. Mickey also felt the routine went well. They enjoyed working together. It was their work, and their contentment.

Waiting for her as she worked, Jack yearned for her and Julie admired her.

"She really is great Jack. I'm glad you didn't settle for anyone else. Either here or anywhere else for all those years." Julie said.

"I know. And I'm glad every day. I'm thankful for her," he admitted.

Julie had never heard him speak like this about any woman. She watched Jack when Michaela was near him. Full of admiration and expectation, he adored her. As Mickey came from the barn, closing the large door for warmth, she walked confidently, as if she were pleased. She wore a smile of satisfaction as Jack climbed the corral and met her fifteen feet from the perimeter. Picking her up under her bottom, he carried her in a circle, admiring and complimenting her precision. The affection and his greeting, were not yet old to her. She hoped they never would be. Whispering unheard words to him, a long kiss followed accompanied by small steps toward the barrier. When they reached the edge of the corral, they turned to invite Julie's opinion. She entered the house, one hundred feet away, ahead of them and alone.

"I have some cake for you two if you would like it. That was very impressive Mick! " Julie said.

Julie leaned on the counter of the kitchen on her elbows. "It's great to see a wonderful routine like that." Julie said.

"I still want to see you race Julie! I've never known anyone who raced in any western competitions." Mickey said. "Cutting in so close and coming out without wasting any space or time; exciting!"

Julie stood placid, neither verbose nor withdrawn. "About like most things, the more you practice, the better you get." she said flatly.

"Which is why she keeps the kitchen to herself and doesn't let me practice cooking!" Jack said defiantly.

Mickey's recalled events and moments when the results reflected the work. She smiled. "I better go brush her down. It's a time after she's calm when we communicate about how we did."

Waiting

"That all you're gonna' take?"

"Yes, Jack. It's all I'll need."

Juliana cinched up Jupiter, her strong and at times, intense Paint Horse. Even though he had been with them on the ranch for five years, only she had ridden him. They knew each other. With a heavy, fleece jacket, chaps, hat and an absent look about her, she picked up the sandwich and water and wrapped them tightly. Riding alone on ranch and range held with it some responsibility. She told him where she was headed, and the path she would take.

"I still don't see why, Julie. You know, the day after Thanksgiving and not much required around here; you just take off. And it's not even warm out."

"You ride the range all the time, Jack. What's wrong with me being by myself for a while?"

Jack shrugged. Well, nothin' it's just weird." The wind gusted enough that he needed a tight fitting ball cap on his head while speaking with her at the gate. Even so, he held it down with an index finger. Dust from the corral blew into his eyes.

"It's forty-two degrees! You don't usually do that near a holiday, by yourself and when it's cold!" He held up a hand against the dust.

"Today I am, big brother. Can you take care of feeding the stock? I know it's my turn for the west quarter. "

Jack waved off the request. "Yeah, yeah sure... but why Julie? Anything wrong?"

She climbed atop her personal ranch horse, who knew her as she knew him. Jupiter turned his head to the left, to gain peripheral sight of Julie. She gave him a slow stroke down his mane as she spoke with Jack. Verbally more subdued than usual, she remained intent sitting in the saddle, even in the wind. Looking downward, gazing at her brother eye to eye from atop Jupiter, she stared blankly at him. Not angrily and not fanciful, just blank.

"Julie, you wanna' take some time off? I can handle the place."

His sister sat there, still looking at him with little emotion. Jupiter appeared pensive. His sister's gaze slowly fell from his face down his six foot frame to where his boots stood, dust blowing across the tops of them.

"You look good Jack, really good."

A gust of chilly wind blew the hair at each side of her face underneath her rust colored riding hat. It was cinched underneath her chin for warmth and to keep from losing it in the wind. The hair at her temples, the hair never long enough to go into a braid, flew wildly.

"Really good! I think Michaela is the reason. Take care of her Jack." She spoke loudly over an increasing gust. Give her everything a woman needs, you know? Can you do that?" Her pensive mood seemed to match the weather.

Jack stood and stared at his younger sister who, ready to head into the low hills eastward on their property and maybe farther, reached out for his hand. A bedroll was tied behind her. He knew it was just a precaution. She grasped Jack's strong hand and held it for only a moment before she put the sandwich and water into a leather pouch in front of her knee.

"Julie!"

"Bye Jack, I won't be long; maybe a three or four hours. If I should have any trouble, lose a shoe or whatever, we'll walk back the same way, okay?" He didn't reply, but stood silent watching the woman who did so much work alongside him ready herself to ride away. It was their ranch, his and hers. He had grown up with her, suffered trouble with her, and had enjoyed a confidant in her for most of his life. He couldn't think of a thing to say.

She gave Jupiter a soft heel in his ribs. Slowly they made off. Julie adjusted her tight fitting hat downward, over her head slightly as they left the grounds near the house. He knew she could take care of herself. Usually she did a better job at responsible living than most of the men he knew, who seemed to be often dependent on someone for something. It was just the timing and her distanced attitude that bothered him. Was she thinking about moving into town? Leaving? He didn't know.

Two hours later, he stood with a cup of coffee, staring at the barn. Missy had seemed to take living at the ranch in stride. He fed her and let her out on days when Michaela couldn't come early enough. Lately there were not many days when she didn't drive out at least for an evening. Leaning on the windowsill, he thought about Julie. He couldn't figure it out. She had been a little testy lately, but she hadn't mentioned anything wrong. After she had been gone more than three hours, he became agitated. She had told him four. He would wait a two more hours and feed the livestock in the meantime.

Jack threw an empty bucket into a bin. Frustrated, he had done all that he came out to do. He walked around the inside of the barn, checked on Reacher and the other horses. Patting Reach solidly, his coat was very cool to the touch. Jack had been out of the house for only forty minutes, but the temperature had dropped. The wind which had been increasing, slowed a little. Walking five spaces to where Missy stood, he rubbed down her coat gently. A fine animal, Jack had decided that he liked the breed. He brushed her with his own brush used for Reacher while thinking of both Michaela and Julie. As he thought, he searched until he found the better brush that Mickey always used for Missy and finished brushing her down. Five minutes into the grooming, Michaela walked into the barn.

"Well... my two favorite personalities! Whatcha doin' there, Jack?"

He gave her a solid kiss, pulling her to him and holding her there. After the kiss, she held him.

"Whatchathinkin' there, Jack?" There was a playfulness in her eye. The playfulness receded gradually as he told her of Julie and their short discussion before she had left. He told Mickey of how she gave no explanation of leaving, but that she just did so.

"How long now?"

"Five hours"

"She said four?"

"Yeah..." he said absently, thinking.

"Thanks for brushing out Missy. Let's go inside."

Cup after cup was poured until the coffee was gone and their conversation was less concluded than ever. "How long now?" Mickey asked.

"Six and change," Jack replied softly.

"Night falls fast this time of year, but I know she'll be fine. You grew up together, you know she will be okay."

Mentally he traced Julie's course. He had made the same journey a hundred times. The range was one place he was possibly more capable than she. It wasn't that far, maybe ten or twelve miles. They could travel it in no time in a truck, except for the gulleys. There were cut outs of land owned by others that lay between what they owned in the hills and at the ranch itself. If she went to the hills, where they both liked to ride, there were many different trails up there she could follow.

Mickey touched his hand. "No worries Jack, she's good on her own, you know."

"And-how, I know! She's been on my case since we were kids. You'd never think that she's the younger one. She's a mothering type."

"She is that!" Michaela said nodding. She took another sip of freshly made coffee.

"Now I am getting concerned!" Jack said nearly an hour later. "It was just weird before, but now it's strange. It's just not something she does. The gulleys are hard to see in at night, if she went that way.

"Look, Jack." Mickey began. "I don't think it's anything to worry about. She and I had a talk a few days ago."

At this, she had his attention. "A talk?"

She ran her fingers up and down the long sleeve shirt he wore.

"Yeah honey, a talk."

"What?" he asked, looking her in the eye.

"Jack, she's lonely. I know she's been coming down on you about finding a wife and everything these last years; and part of that is her mothering nature. But also," she said, stopping mid-sentence.

"Also what?"

"She wants a man of her own. She's waiting, you know? She's been waiting, Jack. She's wondering if she will meet someone. I know she's only twenty-eight, but that's it. She told me the other night that she and I would be friends forever. It was the kind of thing that you say when you need a friend, you know? She's really glad that we, you and I, have so much to share. But she wants the same, that's all. "

He had to admit. It made sense. Julie was a handful, but he could see it happening. He sat his cup down and tapped it on the table, empty.

"I suppose there is a man somewhere that could handle her without taking to drinking, or killing her." he said flatly with a somber face as he stared out the kitchen window in the direction of the barn.

Slapping his arm, "Oh, You! She's not that bad. I like her!" Turning toward Mickey he emotionally attached his thoughts to her. His girl, always captivating, and intelligent too; still missed a few things. He managed a sincere look and a half smile.

"You say that because she never bit your leg!"

Mickey sat up from her relaxed posture at the kitchen table and stretched her legs out under it. She breathed out a small giggle, like a young girl. She rested her chin on the palm of her hand. She looked him in the eye and spoke in a staccato rhythm as she called him on his statement.

"She did-not-bite-your-leg!" Her eyes beamed into him for emphasis. With a wry smile, he assured her that he was right. Pulling up his blue-jean covered leg half of the way to his knee, he positioned his right leg in the light of the kitchen until a small spot of white scar tissue became evident. He held the leg out in front of her, pointing to it but saying nothing.

Her eyebrows went up and her seductive, slightly almond shaped eyes opened wide.

"Julie?" she whispered, questioning him? He yanked down on his jeans and straightened them over his boot.

"YES! Eighteen freaking years ago! She should have known better than to do that, and I should have known better than to trust her with my back turned. If she had been a rattlesnake? He intensified the question by his rising tone. He snapped his fingers to illustrate the point. "Goner, dead meat, road kill.... Julie kill! ".

They laughed loud and long. It did help relieve the tension. Mickey increasingly enjoyed the stories that Jack and Julie told of their life together. They were funny sometimes, sometimes caring, but also they were intriguing.

"I've always wanted a brother myself, like you and Julie are. It's a wonderful thing, Mr. Man!" she dictated, with a finger pointed at him. "I've always wanted that!"

"Oh great! How touching! Next time I'll let her bite *your* leg, then we'll see if you feel the same!"

"Laughter does warm the heart!" Mickey said smiling, to his reply. And it warmed the kitchen until he looked out the window at the darkening night. "It's been over six-and-a-half hours. I'm putting a saddle on Reach. "

She took the opportunity to soften his worries. "There, you see? You do care about her!" He stood looking out the window into the dark. "Sure I care! She's half the labor around here, and a better cook that I am." He said, almost without emotion as he stared out the window. At that, she punched him in the arm with force.

"Alright, I'll help you get everything on Reacher."

With jackets, ball caps and somber thoughts, they set out toward the barn to saddle Reacher, each with their own mood while they walked. Almost to the door, they heard her in the darkness.

"Hey! Hey! Over here!" Turning, Jack and Mickey saw her next to Jupiter both walking toward them and carrying a slight limp. They came into the yard heading toward the barn. Julie's jeans were torn and her hat was gone. A small amount of blood showed through the tear in the jeans. Obviously cold, there were other scrapes that were visible as well.

"Would you take care of Jupiter, Jack? He needs his leg taped. I need some warm coffee."

Not waiting for a reply, she was gone. She headed straight to the house with Mickey following, looking back toward Jack.

As soon as Jack had the leg taped and assured himself that there wasn't serious damage to his sister's pride and joy, he headed back to the house. He walked in as Julie poured the first cup from a new pot of coffee.

"Sis, what happened? I was just getting Reach ready to go out looking for you!" She leaned her head back and rolled it from side to side, eyes closed. Her hair had completely come loose from her usual pony tail, as it hung tangled down the back of the chair. Stretching the neck muscles, for as long as she could stand, she took too quick of a sip of the fresh coffee. It burned her mouth. Slamming the cup down hard, the coffee shot vertically above it, but fell perfectly back into the cup. She leaned forward and put her head down on the table for a minute.

"What happened Julie?"

Sitting up slowly, she looked at them both with squinted eyes, the way she had looked about the dishwasher soap earlier in the week. Jack knew it was coming, something intense was about to be released.

"Julie?" Mickey said softly.

"What happened?" She doubled back to him. "You want to KNOW WHAT HAPPENED?" Both silent, her brother and newly adopted sister both gave a short nod, respecting her experience.

"Well, Jupe n' I were having a nice ride. We would have even been back before dark! We were walking through the hills up there where the trees are tall and there are rocks..." She didn't finish the sentence, instead sipping again.

"Yeah?" Jack asked, pouring her more coffee.

"YEAH? WELL!" she said, agitated while staring at him. He sat back. They would wait for her to continue when she was ready. Another sip did it.

"We were stepping through there nicely. He was sure footed for being up there. You know how it is up there, walking through the rocks. Well this Mountain Lion jumps out from behind a rock screeching like a shop vac. And he would have got Jupiter, except Jupe' fell back on his haunches and I fell off him, right on my ass! I bruised n' hurt my hip and messed up my leg. Well, this S-O-B cat that thinks he's going to get a five course dinner on Jupe' is closing in see..." She took another draft of the coffee while rubbing her leg subconsciously and frowning. "Well, he's making his approach, and Jupe' is all scared, screaming and trying to get up but slipping on the loose rocks. Well, I let that sorry S-O-B cat have it with my pistol and blew a hole in him the

120

size of a watermelon! He won't be freakin' jumping out at us from behind rocks anymore!"

The more she recounted the story, the angrier she got. Julie held her neck and took a breath with her eyes closed, rubbing her head. Mickey stood behind her against the kitchen cabinet with a hand over her mouth at the story, silently laughing at the description of the event; but not wanting Julie to hear her laughter and maybe hurt her feelings. Vehement, Julie readied herself to continue the story.

"That's it?" Jack asked, too impatient to wait. Julie rubbed one eye while opening the other and squinted at him.

"Yeah, that's about all, bub! Except that that stupid cat won't be getting up anymore after I gave it to him in the gut! I shot him four times! AND, after I was sure that he was as dead as Aunt Minnie's Ox, I was still so mad at that piece of ...." She caught herself. "Well anyway, I freakin' bashed his head with a rock and busted out a few teeth out in the process. I was so pissed! Then I buried that rag of a body under a bunch of rocks! That lame, piece of dog crap won't get up again! He hurt Jupiter and didn't do me any good either! STUPID PIECE OF CRAP, S-O-B CAT!"

Jack, quiet now, stared at his sister. In her whole life, he had never seen her this mad. When he finally took his eyes off her while she rubbed her head, he looked up to Michaela who was in the corner of the kitchen. Doubled over in convulsive laughter and barely able to keep silent, she held both hands over her mouth, straining. Her head was turning toward the oven and she was lifting one foot, hunched up from hearing the story. When Mickey looked at him, he held an arm outstretched with his palm up, and raised his eyebrows for emphasis as he pointed to his leg with the other hand. At this, Mickey ran out of the kitchen to the bathroom shutting the door quickly. He thought that he could hear her laughing from forty feet away.

Jack waited for a few minutes before getting up. When Julie was still and seemed to be settling down, he ran water in the kitchen sink, warming it. When hot, he pulled a clean dishrag from the drawer, soaking it in the water. As Julie sat half asleep, occasionally shivering from the chill of walking back nine miles with Jupiter; he gently wiped her head and neck with the warm rag. As he washed off the dirt, sweat and anger, she began to relax. Making it hotter, he held it on her neck. The water soaked into her shirt.

"Mmmm... that's it, right there," she said.

After ten minutes, Mickey returned to the kitchen and approached quietly while Julie half slept in the chair after having drank nearly the whole pot of coffee.

"Can I run you a bath Julie?" she asked caringly, touching her arm. In a flash of thought and slowly shaking his head, Jack mentally compared the two women in his life. They could both handle a horse, both could cook and both were about the same in height and attractiveness. It was temperament however, that was the difference between them. One raw power, the other refined gentility. It had made all the difference tonight.

122

"Yeah, that would be great, chick, " Julie said exhausted, while reaching upward.

Mickey grabbed and held her hand for a full minute, squeezing it periodically. At the kitchen table in front of Julie, the remaining coffee in the pot merely covered the bottom. Julie stood, balancing herself. In front of them both, she unbuttoned her jeans while leaning on the table and pulled them down to her knees. Her leg was stained with blood. While hard to tell without it having been washed yet, the cuts looked clean. The scrapes that had not let blood were also fully visible. A large bruise and cut on her right butt cheek had stained her panties high on her hip where she had fallen. She turned to see her hip, but couldn't.

"Owww!" She rubbed her neck, getting angry again. "STUPID A-HOLE CAT! It was a TOM! And if I had been thinking clearly..." She rubbed her neck again, starting to growl.

"I would have blown his nuts off and give him a *new* A-hole for no freakin' extra charge!"

Mickey convulsed in rhythms again, but managed to merely keep a strong smile and not let out the laughter this time. Standing up and walking slowly, Julie made another pronouncement as she shuffled toward the bathroom. "I'm taking the day off tomorrow guys. I'm sorry I haven't been normal Julie tonight. Right now I'm tired, I'm hungry, I need to pee, and my ass hurts! Goodnight!"

After she had gone he began forming the words for his comment at her exit. Mickey stopped him with a lifted palm.

"Don't say it!" she said.

"Not the NORMAL JULIE? Uugh!" he sighed. "She didn't need coffee, she needed some kind of whiskey!" Mickey laughed out loud. "I knew what you were going to say!" she said. Jack shook his head as he stood up, gazing down at the coffee pot. "Kinda' makes you feel at least a little sorry for the cat."

J J

"She's only my sister, but that's enough. How would you like to be married to that? You might wake up one day with your head bashed in!"

Mickey smiled supportively but dropped her face into her hand. As they sat on the bed in the guest room, she briefly thought of all that had occurred in the last months since she had come to know Jack and Two-Jay. Jack, kind and intelligent, both he and Julie capable in farming and ranching; with the fine life of a family. It was only a two person family. Still, she wanted to be part of it.

Jack looked at Mickey. "You okay? Tired? You look it."

"Yes, but it's more than that. The job at the elevator is fine but..." she said. "Oh, never mind."

"But what?" Jack said.

"It's you and Julie. It's your life. Oh, I don't mean the ranch. That's nice of course, but the two of you! You work together well.

That is, when she's not killing cats."

Jack shook his head again. "The most angry that I've ever seen her. But she's right, a big cat like that could have really messed up Jupiter. Instead of just a sprain, it could have killed him," he thought about Julie again as she bumped two glass somethings together in the bathroom next door. "Man, if that cat would have messed up Jupiter, it would have been hell to pay for everyone." Michaela let her tired eyes fall on the man who had so rapidly won her heart. Maybe it was the trauma of the last hours, maybe it was a longing in her own heart.

"Jack, later...in a few months or whenever; are you going to ask me to marry you?"

Rubbing his face, he stopped suddenly and looked over at her. Her expression was one of sincerity and honesty not humor. Her eyes were kind and peaceful, the look he had always wanted to see in a woman he loved.

"I was kind of planning on it; at some point that is better than a time like this," he smiled.

"Good, because I might need to think about it," she said. She remembered the first time he had come to the elevator to ask her to dinner. He looked around the room thinking, not sure why she had brought this up now. Then he remembered the earlier scene in her office. He smiled directly at her, eye to eye. "It's been a good few months hasn't it?"

"Oh Jack, it's been wonderful. And I want to be your wife. I'm not pushing you, understand that. But some things in life are so special that you can't take a chance on not saying what you should say at certain times. If you *have* thought about it..." she stopped, searching for the right words. "I mean, I'm not the just live with a man, kind of girl. I wouldn't want to miss being married."

Tired also by the holiday and everything that occurred, he nodded thoughtfully. "That's true, you're not. In fact I have never thought of you like that. And I never have thought much of the kind of life where people drift in and drift out. I would never ask that of you, or want that for you Michaela." She knew he was his most serious when he used that name.

"I never would...ask that of you," he said. Tired, he thought hard, concentrating. I mean, you can't have beautiful flowers that you want to grow, and constantly move them around in the ground and expected them to grow well. She pulled her feet up and put them on the railing at the side of the bed. Her chin was in her palms. "I like that! That's good. I'm glad you *are* the marrying kind Jack, I wouldn't want to miss it.

"Well, you just watch your step girl, and maybe you won't!"

She let out a short laugh in an exhale and fell back onto the bed. The fresh scent of the recently washed sheets was strong. Julie was a good housekeeper too, on top of everything else. Jack looked at Mickey lying down in front of him, eyes closed on the bed. Rising slowly, he bent over her and kissed her on the forehead. Slow to speak, she smiled. "Whatcha' doing

126

there, Jack?" It was almost a whisper, like before, but it was one of love. She was as tired as he, but she felt contented. It took less than a minute before she fell asleep. Watching her, he noticed her day clothes. Gently, he undid the button at the top of her jeans, unzipping them as well while looking to her face. She didn't react. He pulled off both shoes but left the socks on her feet as she lay in a light doze. He checked to ensure she wore underwear, and lifting her hips, he slid her jeans down over them and easily off her legs. Appreciating her legs in a tired state himself, he gazed at her. He had never seen them. Like her mind and heart, they were beautiful. Her underwear, a print of English riding horses, fit her. A last, a tired smile spread across his lips as he pulled the comforter from the other side of the bed and laid it over her. When he moved to leave she spoke, barely audible.

"My...and you are a gentleman too. Too hard to come by. Mmmm... Night."

He turned out the light. "Goodnight, Sweetheart."

Julie

"SUUUWHHHEEEEEEEEEAAAAAAHHHHH! WHEEEEEEEEE HAAAAA!"

Julie called out the window of the feed truck. Michaela, off work for the afternoon, due to lower volume at the elevator, cringed as Julie practically screamed at the cattle in the pasture by the fence. She called to them, bringing them hay. The small herd had been scavenging the leavings of mature grass at the fence line. Not enough to feed the small herd of thirty head that remained, the cattle they had kept after the previous season began a slow follow-the-leader, trail of walking beef toward the feeder. Following the fence line until the lead animal turned out toward the round bail feeder, they each followed suit. As Julie drove the farm truck through the field to the feeder and passed it, she put the transmission into reverse to back-up to it. The twelve-hundred pound round bale of field grass, baled late from the recent season was highest in nutrition. It sat high on the rear of the truck, lifted it there by hydraulic force, allowing a large amount of hay to be moved at one time. A necessary food during winter, the circular bale fell with a thud into the round, containment railing that allowed multiple head of cattle to feed at once. Hungry, they were nearing the feeder already. As Michaela rode with Julie, she watched the antics and characteristics not only of the cattle, but of her recently discovered sister of a heart. She hoped Julie would be a sister-in-law one day. Julie could screech, ride, carry hay and cook with the best of them.

"Not that much to look at now, but they will be better in some months," Julie said. "Our family has always range fed. We believe it keeps the cattle healthier and to a large degree makes the meat better. One thing that Jack and I try to do to make the best beef, for us anyway, is to try and give a little extra into the livestock." Julie spoke without asking whether Mickey wanted to hear it or not. It was almost as if she were Jack.

"When we have an odd lot of livestock like this, we try to do things for them to make their lives better. A lot of ranchers would laugh at that, until they taste our beef. I mean think about it! "Julie emphasized her point. "When we are happier we are healthier, and when we are healthier we are happier. Jack and I buy a little sweet alfalfa each year to give them just to perk them up. They can smell it a mile away. It's like candy to them." Not thinking about the fact that Mickey knew cattle, she spoke mostly out of boredom. In fact Mickey knew everything she said about livestock, except for the way that Two-Jay liked to treat them to something pleasant now and then.

"The alfalfa makes them about as happy as they can be. You'll be able to taste that happiness in your steak later in the year.

What goes around comes around, you know?" Julie said.

"Right," Mickey said as she examined their pasture.

"Jack and I and our folks before we lost them, see it this way; kindness, support, caring and hard work, you know, love of God, the land and each other isn't just a part of life. It *is* life! In the old times people wouldn't have survived without those things. And Jack and I, despite my Calamity Jane moments..." She looked over at Mickey who was already smiling and turning her head away with the humor. "...really believe that and have lived it with each other. I mean, since our parents have been gone, our Maker's patience, and Jack's love and that of myself; our support for each other have been the things we've found we can't do without. We drive each other crazy sometimes, but we can't do without it."

"That's beautiful Julie, I hadn't heard you say anything like that in the whole time that I've been here."

"I know, and even Jack and I only talk about it once in a while. For instance, when Jupe' n I came back from our foray into the hills and I was so wiped out; you were in the back and Jack got the water hot in the sink and soaked my neck and shoulder muscles with it. He probably doesn't even think I remember that he did it, but I do. And you there, holding my hand and making up a bath for me. That's the kind of stuff we're about here, Mickey. Why, one time Jack got thrown off a horse that we were working into our stock, and broke one wrist, and fractured the other and an ankle. That was only a year after our folks were gone. I hired a couple of high school kids to do the basics around here, and for the most part, I took care of Jack." At recalling this memory she was quiescent for a few seconds, then burst out into a laughter that she hadn't displayed before in Mickey's presence.

"What? What is it Julie? Tell me."

"You sure?" she questioned Mickey with raised eyebrows, taking the responsibility off her and onto the woman they already saw as a member of their family.

"Yes! Tell me, and don't leave anything out!"

Julie looked at the petite, yet strong horse master next to her. Beautiful, with a sharp mind, who had become a sharer in the work and trials of Two-Jay. She would experience it all herself. She already was a sister.

"Okay, but you asked for it! Back there, when I was talking about when Jack broke both wrists and a foot?" She said, questioning Mickey.

"Yeah." Mickey replied, excited now to know.

"Well, when he was laid up, there was no nurse or anyone here to take care of his...personal needs. You know?"

Mickey's eyebrows went up a little and her eyes widened as she thought. "No... No, I guess not."

Well big, strong cowboy Jack had his chest washed, his hair washed and combed, his little-jack washed and his stinky cowboy butt washed; and there wasn't a darn thing he could do about it!"

Mickey, already laughing out loud, now roared. It was one thing about this family that was clear. Laughter was a healing medicine here." Okay, continue..." she said, through her chuckling.

"Like I said, he couldn't do anything about it. I told him that it was our home and there was no way in Hades that he was going without a bath for no seven weeks until he was healed up. He didn't like it, but every time he protested I hit him. And he couldn't hit back!"

Mickey stomped her feet and pounded the dashboard of the truck. She laughed hard at Jack's expense. "Okay, GO!" she said, encouragingly.

"Same stuff every two days, I dragged his butt into the bath and washed him down like he was a flea-bag dog. When he got out of line, I hit him, hard a couple of times! But he learned. Once, and only once, he got cute with me about me handling his private stuff. Well, he thought he was funny, so while he had his eyes closed laughing at me I grabbed the shampoo bottle and shot soap in his mouth! He was hours spitting and hacking! I put him in his place, that's for sure."

Minutes went by as the two women, who, surprisingly had so much in common laughed their way back to the house during the short drive. Calm enough when they got back to talk, Julie finished the story. "Well, after a few weeks, he just stepped into that bath as naked as a mutt that had just been shaved for the summer; pink as could be! Gradually he got used to it and it was alright." Her tone lowered and she became more philosophical. "No one else in the world knows that story Mickey, but that is what I mean about life here. We have to depend on each other, during hardship or embarrassment or whatever. You know?"

"Yeah, I know. Thanks for telling me that. It means a lot. Not only for the humor, but it helps me appreciate both of you."

"Yeah, and one fun thing about it is; if Jack ever gets out of line, you or I can threaten to tell the people in town about me washing his little winkie and his stinky butt!" Julie threw the gearshift into first, shut off the engine and let the clutch out as they laughed until no energy remained for it. Finally quiet, Julie spoke again.

"Mickey, you're going to marry Jack, I know that. And I have a feeling that once he knows that you know his secrets, he will be a good little hubby for you. And make him take out the trash without back talk." Mickey smiled, knowing exactly what she meant. She shook her head at the craziness of it all and then stopped. She looked over at Julie. Julie stood five feet six-and-a-half inches tall. Although she had a well-proportioned figure, she was just a little thicker through the middle than herself. In all, a beautiful woman in her own right, just two years older. Thinking, Mickey suddenly became curious and prodded her.

"So...was there ever a time when Jack had to help you... like that?" She made a motion toward Julie's middle.

"Sort of, I guess, Julie said. One time I ripped the seat of my jeans, and the seat of my butt by the way, on a nail or some such thing. Well, it was a pretty good cut and it was bleeding badly. The piece of metal, maybe it had once been a nail, I don't remember. It was rusty and Jack was right there. He heard me yell and saw me hobbling around holding my butt. I took my hand off my jeans and it was all bloody. It eventually took some stitches to fix it. Well there was someone else nearby then, and I didn't want it to turn into a big, embarrassing thing, so he helped me into the house and onto the big couch. And according to him at the time, it looked to be cut pretty deep, so he gets a towel and he pulls off my jeans and then my underwear. I mean that little piece of metal gave me a new crack, girl! I had to get a tetanus shot later. So anyway, here I am, his twenty-two year old sister at the time, butt naked down there in front of Jack, of all people. Sooo, he doctors me up with peroxide and alcohol and a bandage; really more like a towel, because the cut was still bleeding pretty badly. But he taped me up. And of course he had to make a few brother comments! I was already mad! Looking back; he was just trying to lighten up the moment you know, I see that now. But then, I didn't care. I mean, IT HURT! It hurt like... well anyway...he said something like; I looked pretty hot down there for a sister."

"And you let him have it!" Mickey said.

"Oh, you have no idea! I swung back and punched him in the head twice and told him that he had to sleep sometime!" Mickey's expression was one of amazement, shaking her head slowly with closed eyes and a smile.

"Later, I felt bad and made it up to him with a good dinner. Because if he hadn't been there for me, it could've been really rough." At that, the two women, of one mind, leaned into each other and found humor, deep solace and friendship in another. Neither had known that before. It many ways for each of them, it was for the first time. Mickey had already become family.

J J

The first Sunday of the week in December, as befitted the season, a light and celebratory mood fell on Redlands. After a fifteen minute drive into town, the mood of a cloudy and very cool day, changed to lightness. Walking downtown at three p.m. allowed all who attended the town center celebrations a chance to share in the atmosphere of those businesses who displayed lights, have a hot cup of cocoa, and hear children's groups singing on selected corners of the Redlands downtown area. Even the bank contributed by giving children one dollar each, in hopes that the child's parents would come in the following week and open a savings account for their kids. The time with others in the town center, reminiscent of times past, still held the local traditions of a small town Christmas. Those who didn't own farms and lived inside the town limits, already had carried a holiday attitude since Thanksgiving. Julie, joining a few other women, some who had husbands and some who hadn't, gathered her own moments of pleasant conversation. Holding hands and keeping a slow pace, Jack walked the sidewalk with Michaela. Sometimes speaking, sometimes not, they were sharing the things that one could not share in the same way if a person were by themselves, or alone; which were not always the same thing. This was a time in the small town that, when possible, is best shared with a companion.

After returning home, the three all contributed to dinner, each cooking part of it. The warm toned cabinetry of the comfortable, wide spaced kitchen put a warm glow in their mood as well. The space allowed for the freedom of movement for all three. Yams, Sweet potatoes, leftover turkey and vegetables were spread on the table. This meal particularly was shared together in a relaxed mood on this Sunday evening without a hectic mindset that was often the case during the week. Things were good. Mickey was thrilled at how Missy appeared to be thriving at Two-Jay, and the livestock appeared at the end of the year, to be healthy and prospering. The light, contesting discussions made their days even better. After a break of conversation in which each person finished their share of the meal with a slow satisfaction, it picked up again as Jack became prodded out of his contentment during the dessert.

"So Jack, my brother, are you happy these days?" Julie offered, nibbling the last of a roll and keeping an even facial expression.

"I guess so...I mean, Mickey makes all the difference. Why?" Michaela's expression became even warmer at his words. He sat, careful with the knife as if it were words, when he sliced a smaller piece of pie than was normal for him. An introduction to a conversation by Julie, said in *that* tone could mean anything. And he could be sure of it now. It had simply been too nice of a day for her to leave it alone.

"Oh, what a sweet thing to say! Anyway, we girls just care about you, Jackie." Now he knew something was up. She was never so nice unless there was a land mine somewhere nearby that he may inadvertently step on; sometimes with a push from behind.

"Yeah, since when?" he said.

"Oh, we just always want you to be healthy and happy, that's all. How do you feel about doing the dishes tonight?" He sighed, and put down his fork after only one bite. It had to be about more than doing dishes. He loved Michaela and he loved his sister; at least as much as a man could love a live electrical wire. Electricity was a great thing when under control, but loose it, and all kinds of horrible things could happen. With the good mood of the season and having been into town sharing the holiday with others, followed by a pleasant dinner, Julie became more like the loose wire. And the current was aimed at him.

"Look... Julie, I've had a pretty nice day so far. You're not going to rain on my evening are you?"

"Why Jack, what an awful thing to say, and at Christmas time too, Tsk, tsk,tsk." Deciding to finish the pie sometime when he could actually enjoy it, he put a simple napkin over it, with the fork on top; waiting for the sucker punch. He looked at Julie. Jack, being reasonably handsome as a man and successful in most ways only made it worse. He was going to get it. Julie sat back relaxed, with one leg over an arm of her dinner chair carrying a straight face. She sat looking as innocent as a newborn lamb. He closed his eyes. Michaela watched her man. She smiled a simple, sweet smile seeming to understand what was happening. Still, she didn't include him in sorting out the puzzle.

"What do you want Julie?" he spoke straightforward and factual, like in a courtroom scene.

"Hmmm? OH, well, it's just that I, I mean we, just thought you might want to do the dishes... for the next TWENTY YEARS!" At that Michaela burst out, leaning over her finished plate giggling, while Julie sat with a sly smile on her face. How had he rated such a sister? She was strong and talented, fierce and dedicated like a bulldog, and even pretty. She was also a snake!

"Twenty years," he replied flatly. "Some significance to that? Am I supposed to serve in the Two-Jay gulag and see if I survive?" Julie, unaware of what the gulag phrase meant, not being as well read as her brother, passed it off. It didn't matter. The electricity was arcing, waiting to kill the vulnerable. And he didn't want to play. He rested his chin in the palm of his hand, staring at her and waiting.

"Jack? You okay buddy?" Julie leaned forward in great, mock

concern. She was having way too much fun. He swallowed hard and turned to Michaela.

"Do you know what this is about?"

"I confess, I do honey, but it's already out of my hands, not a thing I can do, really!" She smiled sweetly; even warmly, seeming to say that once he comes out of this, she will be there for him. He knew that. She would love him always. And that was something anyway.

"Mickey and I had a little talk out on the forty today." Julie said, as she began her final torpedo run. She was positioning herself like a submarine right before an enemy ship gets the 'deep-six'. She continued, restraining her anticipation.

"It seems that there were things that she didn't know about you and I. You know Jack, about how we always take care of each other; about how we are always there for each other." WAR! She had told Mickey. Now there were two women that would hold their edge over him for the rest of his life. They could completely unhinge his future at any time on any day with everyone he knew. He had enjoyed a good day. He had always been to church and been giving and patient, helping people not as prosperous or as gifted as he. He even helped the Boy Scouts now and then. How could it happen? Julie...a sister? Maybe they weren't really related. She could have been left on the doorstep. Or maybe an experimental medicine when she was a child. Nothing made sense of it. He sat silent, staring at the new, shiny black oven in the kitchen ten feet away and directly in front of him. Fire... heat... baking the life out of things. It sounded a lot like hell at the moment. Why did hell always look so shiny and polished when viewed from the outside?

"You didn't," he said blankly, with no expression.

"Oh yes, I did sweetie!" She was like an attorney, an expensive one who relished in the kill. "Now about those dishes. I was thinking that you could do them for me tonight, and also for the next year or so. Then, when you get your head on straight and ask this wonderful woman here next to us to marry you; you could do them for her for the next nineteen years. Or..."

Jack stared at the oven and contemplated his plight. "For the rest of my life," he said softly. It all seemed so strange to him now, sitting at the table in the kitchen of the gulag. Juliana had always sounded like such a pretty name.

Christmas

He came in the door of the kitchen with a look. "It's hard to believe that it's this cold only a week before Christmas!" Jack said, after three hours work on the small, feed tractor.

"The barn isn't that bad, but it still gets to you." Julie wondered what the look that he carried meant. "You okay Jack? What's is it?" When he didn't answer, she tried again.

"Do we suddenly have too many bills or something?"

"No, nothing like that." But still he didn't disclose what weighed on his mind. "Did the mail come?" he asked.

"Yeah, on the desk. But I haven't gone through it. And Mickey's here."

"Mickey? Where?"

"Out with Missy. You going out there?"

"Yeah, it's been a while since I checked on Missy anyway."

"Well check on Mickey too, I think she had a hard day at work." As he walked across the yard toward the barn, he wrapped his heavier, leather coat around him. Having just begun getting warm in the kitchen, it was back into the cold. He would see how the two girls were doing. The door didn't make its usual popping sound as he opened it, and he was able to close it again with no noise as he heard Mickey speaking. She was brushing the gleaming Saddlebred slowly and contemplatively as she spoke to the animal.

"Oh Miss! What are we going to do? You are looking great, but this whole winter thing and not knowing what to do for Jack, has got me down." Communication clearly showed through the responses to her rider. There, in spite of the human-animal barrier there was a kind of communication knowing between them, for Mickey's sadness. The horse seemed to feel something. Such is the communication of those who are so close to their animals. She continued speaking softly to Missy while brushing her down slowly.

"Miss, what can I tell Jack? I've never told him everything about me. I mean, I love him and I know he loves me. But how can I ever tell him? Besides that, what can I give Jack? He's not demanding, and he's got everything he wants. I'm pretty sure we'll be together always, but that doesn't help the now, does it?" Jack watched closely. Amazingly, the horse actually was more passive and subdued as she raised her head or tail slightly in a short bob, up and down. It indicated a close, heart connection to each other. It bothered him a little that she had something that she felt so deeply about, that she hadn't told even him. "He wouldn't ask about it. It was the kind of thing no one answers directly anyway. The horse seemed to appreciate the long brush strokes of differing pressure that Michaela gave.

"Missy, you are the only thing I've ever wanted so badly as to be with Jack. The thing I'd really want is to stay here, in the guest room from now on until... I know Jack is too much of a man to let things get out of hand between him and me; though I'm not sure I'm up for that test. How I love him Missy! I've never loved another person that much, ever!" The brushing stopped as she stood close to the award winning horse and ran her hand slowly down its back, while leaning her forehead onto the animal. "Don't tell anyone girl, but I think I love him more than you. Silly of me isn't it, Miss. I love you sweetheart. You and I are going to go into that next competition and you're going to show those other horses who the top-kick is, that's for sure! Matchless is a fine horse, a lot like you. But he doesn't have the canter that you do. We hope the judges can see that. "Wireless is really good isn't she? We'll have to work on oblique walking a lot, just to practice. We'll put your hair up fine when we do that, okay? Do you need eye drops? Mickey pulled her friend's face to her gently. No, I don't think so. I think you are fine now."

Jack stood five stalls away, watching them over the walls

of each stall in between them. Standing in a shadow that the lights cast when on and careful not to move, he had trapped himself. He couldn't let her know that he had heard, not now. Yet he couldn't leave for fear of the door creaking. She brushed repeatedly. She brushed now not for Missy but for herself; with nervous energy.

"Well, that's about it for you. I'd give you more oats, but you can't founder. Neither of us can founder. Pray for me Missy! Silly of me isn't it...I'm glad no one heard me say that, but I believe you know I have something important in my life."

"Jack!" Julie called, as she threw the barn door open. "Jack? You in here?"

"Just me Julie," Mickey called back. I'm just finishing Miss here. Can I help you in the kitchen before I go back to my place? Jack said he might be gone when I came tonight. I guess he was." As Julie walked through the center aisle of the barn, she noticed Jack standing back, half of the distance of the barn away from Mickey in the partial shadow. He quickly held up a finger in front of his lips and motioned for her not to tell Mickey that he was in the barn with them. He gave her an imploring look. She received it with what appeared to be understanding. At least she nodded anyway. That was refreshing. Sometimes she could be human. Sometimes even she got a little more humane during the Christmas season.

As Julie walked past him, she gave him a 'thumbs up' sign with her near hand, and went forward to see the two in the center of the barn.

"Jack should be back any time. Missy okay?" Julie asked.

"OH SURE! She's awesome! We were just talking about winning our next competition." As Mickey put the coat brush into a uniquely made leather bag made for it, she began walking back with Julie, slapping the dust off her hands. As they passed the stall where Jack had been, Julie glanced in his direction enough to ensure whether he was there or not. He had left through the partly open barn door while Mickey was distracted. When they arrived at the kitchen door Jack stood, sorting through the mail.

"Jack!" Mickey half skipped to see him." Somehow it had been good to hear her honest, inner thoughts about how she felt about everything. He knew now that he felt clear about marrying her, it was just a matter of time as to when, and when to ask her. And it also mattered whether she would be okay about what bothered her. She looked him in the eye. "How are you?" she asked, her brown eyes, full of affection.

"I'm a bit cold, girl. You alright?" he asked, as she ran her arms inside his coat to his back.

"I'm fine Jack, Missy is fine. I'll warm you up! I've missed you terribly today, I don't know why. "

"Maybe it's because you like me?" She made a face as she looked up, and reached to kiss him intensely, truly. Julie pulled five almost ready sandwiches out of the refrigerator. She spoke without excess of emotion. "If you two lovers want some grub, I'm going to get a shower. I'm still a little sore after all this time!"

J J

Sipping coffee on the large, leather sofa, Jack listened to the rundown on Mickey's day. The Christmas tree shone steadily in the large den of the house where it sat ten feet from the fireplace. As Mickey spoke, he thought, reflecting on what he had heard in the barn. He listened to her, not only with his ears, but with his eyes. She spoke about everything she had been thinking in the afternoon. He began to think about all the days they had spent together. He wandered with her, story by story. Then, at an unexpected moment, he took another mental road imagining them together for life. Mickey, speaking in a flow like a faucet while he thought, finally turned off.

"What do you think Jack?"

He came back from where he was. The room was warm. She in front of him, just as warm, and his heart's desire. He had lost track of the conversation. "Well? What do you think about it?" She repeated.

"About which? You covered a lot of ground," he said, after being distracted by his own thoughts.

"About my raise, silly?"

"Oh, that! I think it's great! And I'm proud of you." He looked her in the eye, not turning away. He hadn't even heard that she'd gotten a raise. She could sense something. She could feel him reaching for her inside, for her heart.

"Michaela..." Jack said. She smiled. She had gotten used to him switching names when he wanted to talk seriously. She thought it a little funny, but she liked it.

"Michaela... stay here. Stay here with us. Stay with Julie and with me, all the time. You could stay in the guest room, it would be fine that way. We'll be fine, you know with Julie... she will be a good chaperone," he joked, but figured that it wouldn't hurt. The last thing he wanted was to sound corny when talking about the two of them. But the first thing he wanted was her. He smiled his most convincing smile. It was the first smile he had given her, their first day, in her office. It was what he had used trying to interest her at first. He hadn't used it with her in ages. Then, giving more thought about Julie chaperoning them, he felt grim, even depressed. She could! She would! He couldn't imagine a more irritating catalyst in his love equation with Michaela. Julie would mess with them, or at least with him! Not out of nobility or to be some kind of righteous influence; she would be annoying just to mess with him on a day-by-day basis. Whenever the mood struck her. And without realizing it, Jack's thoughts had slipped back into verbal speech as he continued.

"She could kill us both and then go make a meatloaf dinner! Do you realize that?" Mickey laughed and pushed at him.

"My Gosh Jack! What are you talking about? I can't believe you said that."

"Okay," he said, "a revised plan is, that we fool around... a little." Her eyes lit up, becoming enlivened. You know, have some fun when the warden isn't around, but between you and I, we keep it on the level; not too much fun... see? I want to have the best to look forward to, okay?" He walked through his words, like muck boots in a muddy field. "We'll just have to watch it!" Mickey gave him a sly eye. "Okay, I'll have to watch it!" he said.

After having heard the story of the Cougar, she snickered quietly with him. And turning her head toward the kitchen in hopes that Julie hadn't heard the exchange between them, she reached for him. She had more respect for him than ever, but also more desire than ever! As he continued, not realizing that she had already given her answer, actively or passively. He tried again. "Mich... Honey, please stay here with me. You know everything will be fine."

"So then, you won't be um... forcing yourself on me?" she said, with both a smile and the bluntness of a hammer.

"Well, I wasn't going to put it like that, but...yeah, I guess so. It would be the romantic thing to do, and the erotic thing to do." He looked at her smiling. "And it would be the bull-like thing to do." She outright laughed quietly. Then he looked her sharply in the eye and gripped her firmly on each shoulder, lifting her slightly from her firm seat on the couch. "But it's not what I want for you, for us." He relaxed his hold on her and leaned back somewhat, looking at the ceiling, tinted red and green in the semi-darkness from the lights of the tree.

"All my life, I've pushed, strived for the best, you know?" He relaxed his expression and added a smile. "I'm sure you do know, winning with Missy like you have!" She smiled warmly at his pride in her that had stayed strong, and not faded from the first date. "But Michaela, I've also waited for the perfect woman! The perfect woman for me. He stood now, deeply acknowledging with body language what he felt.

"I hate settling, on anything! I hate it! My father taught me that. Life is too short to bungle it up by going halfway or getting lazy. I'm not a couch potato kind of guy. Life...out there..." he waved his arm, seeing through the wall of his home. "Life out there is HUGE! There is more to do and learn than a person could learn in a hundred lifetimes. But we only get one, and it's a short one Mickey!" Now he was reflective. This wasn't the well-read cowboy speaking to her now, it was Jack, the man she had come to love.

"Stay with me here, with Julie. She loves you too. Besides, Missy is here, and you're out here every day anyway. I plan on asking you Michaela, at the right time, the *Right Time*. I won't settle on that either. Until then, you can stay in the guest room." She stood up, in her winter shirt, work jeans and rough work boots. She began a slow strut around the room.

"You mean, then... Mr. Gentner, that you won't try to um... get to anything you might...um..want? You know cowboy, GET

YOUR BULL ON!" He laughed, reaching for her. Gripping her by the shoulders with a smile, he looked into her eyes with an intense expression.

"Don't press your luck!" he said in mock intimidation. She responded by a gentle, knowing look, a serene look. Not humorous or dramatic, serene and peaceful. One that melted his resolve. He closed his eyes and held them shut. "No, honey, I'll want to. I'll want to! I'll want to every minute of every day. But I won't. I know you were kidding there, and it's funny! But... I um always keep my word, you know? He threw it in for relief. Her expression broke, recalling their first encounters in her office when he asked her to dinner. Expressive and smiling large, she replied with a quiet sincerity in her heart. Not giddiness, not Christmas feeling, it was a knowing. A knowing that comes from having sought the life she had wanted for years. Part of that life had been found with Missy, but the most important part, in human terms anyway, had still been missing. But it had arrived now. She was becoming convinced of that.

"Okay Jack, I'll stay." It was all she could want for now. He was used to getting the best in life, and wanted it. And so did she.

J J

Christmas morning, afternoon and evening...they spent together. For two hours, beginning in the early morning, unusual for them both, they watched television sharing a movie and

150

popcorn. Each voiced their opinions on what the main characters of the movie set in North Africa, would do. Throughout the day Mickey would repeatedly give him instruction on backgammon, or he would show her the finer points of chess. He admired her logical mind, as much as her feminine wiles.   With Julie, the three of them, between preparing courses for the Christmas meal, would attempt to sing carols with musical accompaniment by a toy harmonica. It had been given to him by a young boy whom he had taught how to handle sheep. The meal preparations were shared. After eating together, they balanced the conversation with phone calls. Mickey's mother, normally in Carson on Christmas, was absent this year while visiting friends, states away. Closeness was what each of them wanted. Jack and Mickey, not wanting this first Christmas to be for them in any way, cliché', agreed to wait on gifts and concentrate on each other. Julie was merely glad to have a sister in her life that she had never had. Glances, smiles...warm ones that go deeper than the moment, were given and received by everyone. They were the kind of smiles known by people who have been in a family for a lifetime. These good times weren't sappy, they were real. In some way, they had been missing from each of their lives, for all their lives. They were the kind that come from a knowing closeness with each other.

At the end of the evening meal, Jack sat at the kitchen table munching a few saltine crackers. He remained quiet until both of them noticed he wasn't speaking much. Julie dug for an reason.

"What's the matter, Cracker-Jack? Mickey got your tongue?" Michaela giggled out loud *and* smiled inside. He did indeed have her mouth, her kisses and the rest, whenever he wanted them. But it was he that waited, for the best! And in all of her days, all her life afterward, she would remember that and be a fiercely devoted wife and lover because of it. Jack, not to be distracted from a private plan, remained quiet. Not upset, he was quiet. He sat, finishing his slice of pecan pie. And wiping his mouth, he waited.

"Jack?" Mickey searched him, reaching over to rub his arm. "You okay?" He looked over at the most special person in the world to him, and winked.

"Whatcha-say Jack? Are you little boy blue today? It's Christmas, you know." Julie added. Still he sat...waiting.

"Jack! What is it?" Julie asked plainly. At which he replied slyly, looking directly at his sister.

"I'm fine! I just have something for you for Christmas dear sister. I wanted to show you how much I love you!" Wary of his unusual approach to her, Julie began to squint at him. She would draw it out of him if it took all night. "Well? You gonna come out with it, or do I have to serve you up some kind of tongue loosening libations?"

He had been ahead of her, and he was ready. She was curious as he brought out a box smaller than a loaf of bread but about as long. "It's a gift, for you Julie," he spoke kindly, as he handed it to her. Wrapped in glossy, red paper and wrapped neatly, she warily took it from him. She tried hard to read in his face what it meant as she gave the required reply.

"Well, um... thanks Jack. Should I open it now?"

"Oh certainly, I want to see how it fits you."

As Julie slowly opened the package, tearing off the wrapping, she looked at Jack, guessing his motives. "Is this a nice gift, Jack? Or am I going to have to fix you up some cold tapioca, huggy brother?" Michaela, knowing what the box contained, dropped her head in the moment. Sometimes it was nice being on both sides. A girl got the best of everything! Especially the humor. As Julie pulled the final piece of paper from it. Her facial expression changed quickly to one of stern resolve. But because of the day she acquiesced. Before her, on a finely painted black, enamel base, stood a miniature diorama of a mountain lion in the wild. Accompanying it, was a small piece of fur worked neatly into the scene at the bottom.

"It's from your buddy boy. That's a piece of his hide! I thought you might want to remember your exploits, your travels," he said, convulsing in restrained laughter at first, then changed quickly, coming into the open. Her answer was slow and thoughtful.

"I love you too, Jack. Just remember, what I did to him, I could do to another..." she mumbled into her hand indiscernibly, then took the hand away to complete the sentence "... animal!"

"Aww gentle sister! Your warmth inspires a sonnet." Jack said, in an easy way as he stood from his seat to pour a cup of coffee. "Maybe I'll write one for you the next time I'm on the range. He had always had a knack of putting words together well. Let's see," he posed, standing at the kitchen counter staring upward and holding the coffee.

"A woman of the west, she always and forever knew best; she ran rough and ran tough, usually riding alone. One day on the run, her hand on the gun, she met the man of her dreams; they looked at each other as he wanted her- Brother! He wanted all, all that she couldn't give. She with her pony as in life so stoney, one of them just couldn't live! An ill-fated romance, that hadn't a chance; he gave his all, for the gun packing maul, and ended as man of her dreams. She killed the cat and sold his hide, and in that she became a woman of means!"

Acting thoughtful after the poetic jibe, he reminisced.

"Hmmm...Well... I'll work on it!"

Julie rose slowly, lifting the coffee pot, on this Christmas evening together. She filled his cup and leaned back on the counter next to him holding the pot. In her western Christmas blouse she moved close. She acted romantic with a false humor, even seductive in front of their audience. Both women, his sister and the one who would be his lover; though they rarely confessed it in front of him, felt his presence in the home. Not just a physical strength, but an intellectual, almost spiritual one. Eyeing him up

154

and down, Julie spoke. "That's beautiful Jack, how come you and I never got together?" He looked to Mickey who watched expectantly, curious about his response. Then, glancing at his sister who, maintained the charade, Jack looked between each of them repeatedly, eyeing each woman for a moment. Then, staring at the model on the table, he took a sip, and answered.

"Are you kidding? Because I would have ended up like him!"

♩ ♩

The New Year began with a very cold day for western Nebraska, Kansas and Oklahoma. It rapidly became the cold kind of day that makes you wonder what the year will hold. As Julie was in the field with the cattle, Jack fed each of the horses in turn, kept in the barn now from the cold. He examined each one as he fed them. Most of the five horses at Two-Jay Ranch were of average value. Most of them were only ridden a lot when periodic round ups were required to get larger herds of cattle to a corral so they could be loaded in trucks and taken to auction. They were ridden otherwise just enough to keep them used to working. Jack stood in front of Reacher, who when inside like today, found himself more uneasy. Reach had been so much of a help to Jack since becoming his prime horse, that he had come to think of him in the way that Mickey thought of her Saddlebred or the feeling Julie had for Jupiter. Desiring to work, Jack placed him next to Jupiter in the barn, because he calmed somewhat, having a type of animal bond between them. Reliable as far as

Quarter Horses go, Jupiter was Julie's. He belonged now and always had belonged to Julie alone. No one rode him, not even Jack. As he gave Reacher half of an apple, a once weekly gift, like sugar, Jack rubbed his cheek. With Reach' distracted, Jack examined Jupiter. The second half of the apple went to the Paint. As Jupiter ate, Jack checked the taped leg. Considering him top to bottom, Jupiter looked recovered. Julie would defend him against anything. Jack's echoes reverberated in the barn from laughing out loud for the tenth time as he recalled the story of how she had defended him against the mountain lion. "You are okay Jupe'!" Jack said, straightening up. He had examined Jupiter's four hooves and cannons for the second time in a week.

Jack thought as he moved around. It had become something he always did when working, especially when alone or feeding livestock. It had been wonderful having Michaela in the house for the last week. Living with them as she had, even though she had her own room and maintained her job at the elevator, it had been like a fresh breeze in their home. His resolve had increased lately. "We won't wait much longer," he said, to Julie's Paint Horse, allowing his words to become audible.

"Not much longer to wait for what?" he heard Julie ask as she walked into the barn, nearing them as Jack stood with her horse.

"Huh? Oh, I was just telling Jupe' here that it won't be much longer before I ask her to marry me. I wanted to give it time, but I haven't come up with any reason not to marry her." Julie moved close to Jupiter and turned over the idea alongside him.

"No, I don't think so either," she said, leaning on the stall railing and running a hand over the bridge of Jupiter's nose. "Not a thing." As Julie pulled a blanket off the wall of the barn, and slid it over Jupiter, Jack became convinced that she had been more despondent since Christmas. Since Mickey had taken over one of the rooms in the house as her own, Julie had become slightly more quiet and withdrawn. Though it saved Michaela money and she could work with Missy on days when home, it had been a daily reminder to Julie that she had no one in her life.

Jack's real and best reason for him wanting Mickey on the ranch, is that he could hear her voice and feel her near him. As he thought of Mickey's words about how his sister wanted a companion of her own, he tried to lighten Julie's mood.

"Julie, do you think a husband of yours would want to live here, at the ranch, and maybe help expand the place? You two could build your own place and everything." She looked at him blankly. She had never considered that scenario. "I... I don't know Jack. I'd have to think that out, I guess."

"Well, no time like the present to think about it, before you get to that point, right?" she shrugged, still leaning on the railing of the stall. "I guess."

"Hey Julie." Jack became real. What is it? What is bothering you? And don't say *nothing* because I know there is; so give!"

She held her thoughts for a minute as he completed minor cleaning around the barn. Finally she spoke.

"It's just... do you think I will get a man? By that, I mean a real man, not a clunker like that guy from the city." Instantly laughing, then just as quickly apologizing as she made a face, Jack came alongside her.

"Of course, Julie. It just isn't an exact science. You may have to grind off some rough spots on him, or he with you."

"But, I mean I'm twenty-eight. That's getting up there for a girl that has never really been, you know, tight with a guy. The few guys around here that I spent time with didn't add up to much, and that one *dude*, from the city who acted interested, only ended up talking about how much money he made." Jack nodded quietly. He had to agree on that one. "Yeah, you have a point there, there aren't many men around here that will measure up to a fine woman," he said. She made an odd face at her brother.

"Are we still talking about the same thing? Are we still talking about me?" At that Jack popped a little.

"I'm not having any of that kind of talk, you hear? No more! You are amazing Julie, if a bit too intense!" She smiled at his words; the words only family could say and get away with it. But he pressed the point home.

"Look Julie; I was only half kidding months ago back there when I said that if you weren't my sister I'd marry you. It sounds kind of funny maybe, but the meaning is there. You are strong, talented and good looking; the right guy will snap you up like that!" He snapped his fingers hard and fast." Then pausing, he spoke slower and more softly, allowing his words to resolve in her mind. "That is... if you let him."

"What? What do you mean?" she said. Jack thought quickly, but spoke slowly. He knew firsthand what it was like looking for a life mate, especially in Redlands. It wasn't the great pantheon of strong, near perfect men.

"I think the one thing that has kept some men away so far is that, well... in some ways you don't leave a lot for a man to do for you. Understand?" She thought for a minute.

"I guess so," she said. "You mean I've got to be more of a helpless female type. I don't think I can do that, Jack!" But he shook his head. "No, not really that. I mean, a lot of men really respect you, I even know some of them. But they wouldn't want to compete with you. You wouldn't leave them much to lay claim to in life." He leaned on the rail next to her, pulling some loose hair back behind her ear.

"Hmmm, I hadn't thought about it. Maybe you're right," she said.

"Of course I'm right!" Just loosen up a little and be a woman! You're certainly good looking enough. And I've even seen your best as..." He changed his choice of words. "I've seen your best attributes; both capability-wise and even your little pink butt!"

159

She rose up from leaning on the rail. "You lookin' to get punched again, Jack?"

"THERE! YOU SEE?" He pointed it out to her. "I'm trying to compliment you from the standpoint of knowing you better than anyone, saying you're talented and pretty, and you are getting worked up on me again."

"Well, I ... yeah, I guess...sorry."

"You are an awesome girl and a great rancher! I wouldn't begin to compete with you in a race for the barrel; or the kitchen for that matter. Just be a tiny bit needier once in a while. Allow a man to share some of the challenges in life. You might even put on a dress a few times a month and go into town." She made a face, looking like he had an infection that she needed to help treat. "A dress? Are you alright?" she asked flatly, turning her gaze to Jupiter. Jack glanced at her and put away the last of the feed. Remaining still before slowly coming alongside her, he kissed her on the cheek softly."

"I'm fine, Juliana. Are you?"

He would have to ask that! That cut to the center of her being. No, in fact, she wasn't alright. She wanted a life with a man that she understood, and who understood her. She had been lonely for so long, too long.

"Okay, thank you Jack, I'll try to be more um... helpless."

Almost speaking, he felt the need to correct her believing that she had misunderstood, but he didn't. Maybe the weight of what he had said would take effect, somehow. She stroked the cheek of Jupiter. Why weren't men like horses? She wondered. That was something she understood. She managed one last reply to his words.

"Why should a girl have to tone down her abilities just to have a man in her life? Can you give me an answer to that?"

Jack thought and answered understandingly. "Because by *sharing* life, there will be not only the successes to share, but there will be more challenges that will require both of you. And in the process there will be greater satisfaction and more success overall than you ever could have by yourself. Understand?"

She stood still. In one quick breath, she answered. "Let me think about it, you want a casserole or hamburgers tonight?"

Grade 'A'

Michaela came into the morning lit kitchen at ten minutes before eight As she poured orange juice into a glass, she looked at Jack who studied the books for the farm as well as the financial records for the ranch.

"Good Morning, beautiful!" he said.

"Aww, beautiful yourself! What ya' doin?"

"I'm going over the books. I have to see a friend today about possibly going into business together. He runs a dairy and is very good at it. If you feel up to it, I'd like you to come and sort of give me your thoughts on the whole thing. I value your insights."

"That's a nice thing to say!"

He shrugged. "Oh, didn't mean it to be; it's more of a fact than a compliment." He said, distracted as he read.

"Okay, but what's it about?"

"I have this friend who runs a dairy. Like I said, he's good at it, and has made money for years. He's thinking of expanding. And rather than him making payments on a loan, I was considering investing the money he needed to expand, and then I, or I should say *we*, would get a percentage of his monthly gross each month on the addition of the dairy that we would help fund. Whatever he sells, we get a piece of the overall, see?"

"How does Julie see it? I mean, she's the *we*, right?"

"Yeah, sort of; she's busy today, but it would really be my money that I'm investing, not hers or the general ranch money. So really the *we*, is you." Mickey looked at him questioningly.

"Me, Jack?" She finished her orange juice and sat on a bar stool as he explained further, amused that she didn't understand that he was speaking of her.

"When you and I, begin living properly, I mean, when we reach the right," he paused.

"Time," she interjected.

"Yes, that's it. The right *time*, and we would live like loving, intimate spouses which really can't be too soon for me..." he smiled. "Living closely instead of like in a college dormitory, then it would affect you as well since you would be an owner also. Well, of my half anyway."

"I'll be glad to give you my thoughts or views. But I'm sure you know that I support what you think."

"Let's go take a look. It's about that time."

During the twenty minutes and nineteen miles to the Brynn Dairy, she questioned Jack about investment amount and percent return, amortization and risk. She showed a fine mind for business. It made him appreciate her in new ways. "Where did you learn those things?" He asked, curious. "Partly my dad, but partly the cost of a performance, competition horse."

"Of course!" he said, in a matter-of-fact way as they drove onto the dairy. Everything looked neat and clean on the dairy grounds. The yard was well kept and the buildings looked maintained.

The introductions over and some small talk made, Wilson, or Will, began the tour.

"Ask any questions you like, Jack. I know it's been a while since you've been here." Mickey noticed everything as they stepped into the room where the processing began and Wilson, a pleasant and sandy haired man in his mid-thirties began explaining.

"We get up around four-thirty in the morning. If they sleep late, I wake my boys about five. Mornings like today, when it's cold and dark; they put on their chore clothes with coveralls, which they have already worn during the week. They get pretty perfumed by the work," he said, holding a smirk. "Sometimes

they smell like cattle, sometimes milk or just plain shi...um crap."
He said, glancing at Mickey. "When they get milk replacer on
them, it's not so bad. Kind of a nice smell, I think. We use
replacer to supplement what the calves need, because we are
gathering the milk from the cows, of course. He added extra
detail to the tour he would normally give, because Mickey was
new to it, and because they were talking about an invested
percentage. He continued, opening another door.

"You have to have rubber boots here... buckle em' down and
all. You're pretty sleepy at this point sometimes, and you have to
carry a flashlight for outside."

"My daughter has to help too, like the boys, unfortunately. She
doesn't like it simply because you just can't really wash the milk
barn smell out of your hair in just a few minutes. She gets a little
teased about it from the other girls, and I know it's hard for her...
But," he said, raising his hands in the air.

Then he got serious. "Jack, Mickey; this is a Grade 'A'
dairy. It's pretty strict, all the rules that we have to follow. We
have inspectors come and if something isn't right, they'll get ya'.
We milk about sixty cows per day. We can't have any chickens
around because they carry disease. We have only Holsteins
here, they're good milkers. We perform artificial insemination at
our dairy just to ensure we get good calves and keep a good
bloodline." Jack glanced at Mickey, observing her as she took it
all into her head or notebook. She would be impressed with the
intensity and specific efforts that Will made at the dairy. Will

kicked a roll of tags on the floor over to the wall and out of the way as Mickey made notes. Will demonstrated the system as he spoke. "We have the barn here, set up with a holding pen using two sliding doors we can open from the inside that allowed three cows to enter on each side of what we call the 'milk parlor'. The depression in the floor down there puts us at a level of the cow's bags for easier milking. Each cow has a corresponding feeder chute that we can drop food through." He demonstrated as he pulled a cord, which allowed a measure of feed to fall into a trough. He stopped suddenly while on a roll in his presentation. "One good cow we have, her name is Maisy. She's smart and nicely disposed. She has figured out how to pull on the cord herself. So she pretty much helps us in here! Funny things you see..." he said, in a light tone. "There are however another pair of cows we call the "Sisters Scheiss." They both understood, smiling. "They both crap all over everything, and wait until they get in here, in the cleanest part of the place to do it!" He slapped his sides in simulated exasperation. Wanting to bring it to a close, he continued so he could complete work that was already in progress.

"There are sprayer hoses at each station to wash the cows bag and teats with and the milkers hung on a hook by the person doing the milking. They're put on after the bags are washed. The milk flows through the hoses into the glass tubing that you see. It runs along both sides of the room into a big glass dome or 'bubble' as we call it that has a float in it. When the float reaches a certain level, it empties into another tube that carries the milk directly to a cooler that is has to be in a separate room. The milk is never exposed to the outside environment. That is a key thing in a Grade 'A' Dairy. You see all kinds of things in a lower grade dairy. For us, everything has to be painted white so inspectors could see the slightest speck of cow crap or even flies on the wall. Everything is power washed after milking, with the milkers being cleaned and sterilized. The holding pen is scraped and cleaned. The grate and pits that hold the cow crap are hosed and cleaned. Baby calves are bucket fed each morning and evening with milk replacer." He paused a moment. "I like the smell of the stuff," he said, smiling. "It's kind of like malted milk. Usually, I have one hand in a calf's mouth while feeding another. They're pretty tame in here. I finally built a small set of stanchions to get the calves' heads in so it would run more smoothly. We can really move em' now. Both Jack and Mickey still showed interest, so he kept explaining the day's details for each of them.

"Mornings: up at five-thirty. Feed the calves. The kids eat, then come back in and help milk until time to get ready for school. Afternoons are pretty similar guys; you know how farming is. The kids off the bus at about four-thirty. They eat a snack, and then they're back out to bucket feed the calves. Our dogs help bring the cows in from the pasture to milk.

Sometimes cleaning up seems to take forever. The kids start on homework before supper and then we each watch a little TV before bed which is about eight-thirty for us." Continuing his presentation, Mickey looked at Jack, shaking her head at all the procedures that had to be in place in Grade 'A' work.

"Anytime the cow's bags can get mastitis, and when it's cold, the teats can sometimes crack. When that happens we need to treat them with bag balm and that quarter would have to be milked by hand because you wouldn't want balm or blood to be in the milk." He wiped his forehead as he explained in a dramatic way. "If that ever happens, the whole cooler would have to be dumped. That's an eight-hundred gallon cooler back there guys! So we are very careful."

Mickey watched the handsome, if a little heavy, friend of Jack's explain in detail every aspect of the dairy. He finished his marathon of words explaining that most medicines are administered by the family on site.

"Well, that's about it guys. I hope it wasn't dull."

Mickey and Jack looked at each other in appreciation of what they'd seen. "Not at all Will, we appreciate it! I'll talk with my boss here on the way home, but I think we have something that will work well."

On the way back Jack and Mickey spoke on a level that they never had before.

"The fine details of animal husbandry in the production of something perishable like milk is fascinating," Mickey said, with a new appreciation of the process. Jack replied with a characteristic detachment. "Yeah, Will is a hard worker and knows his stuff! What do you think, honey? Should we help him expand?" She thought carefully, staring out the window as the miles went by. He let her have time to think, not rushing her conclusion. "I think it's a good idea, she said. "And I took a lot of notes too!" She held up the pad as Jack laughed out loud, happy at his good fortune in selecting a woman in his life that was not only capable and beautiful in his eyes, but also had a good business mind. "Done deal!" he said, after hearing her words. He held her hand and they remained silent the rest of the drive back into Redlands.

Stopping at one of only four flashing, yellow traffic lights in Redlands, two teenage boys walked quickly by in front of the truck. Both recognized Jack and one saluted him, military style.

"Hey Mr. Jack! Have a good one sir!" Mickey watched the scene as it occured, the whole event passing in an instant.

"Those boys seem to like you," she said. He smiled as he watched the two walk away across the street. "Does everyone in town like you that much?" she asked. He shrugged. "They're Hanson's boys. They work hard and are decent guys...they're alright. I hope my boys will be that polite one day, whenever I have them. It pays to respect people. You never want to make an enemy by accident."

Neither said another word as they drove through Redlands. Driving the section road to Two-Jay, Mickey sat lost in thought as she stared out the window. She sat amazed that everyone she had seen or met since she moved into the area had respect for the man she loved.

Distance

One-Hundred-Eighty miles with a stock trailer behind him and frozen sleet in front of him, covering the road as it fell, put some meaning to the word patience. The engine increased and decreased in tone in no particular pattern. As the sleet lightened up and the road became more passable, he accelerated. When slickness became a problem, he had to slow down. It was common sense, but not necessarily easy. The sixteen head of cattle he had sold to a ranch northwest of Two-Jay, would be delivered in two loads. The eight head that Jack held behind him in the trailer were worth twenty-thousand dollars, even after the offset of a partial trade with the farm, for some machinery he would pick up when he delivered the cattle.

"Problematic," Jack said to himself as he drove alone. Normally he never made a trip like this when weather was expected. But the reports had been for gradual clearing and time had mattered. Winter wheat had already been planted in September, just before he had his first date with Mickey. Selling

170

eight thousand bushels of wheat in November that he had kept binned waiting on better prices, helped. He received a little over forty-thousand dollars from it, Jack had sustained a positive account balance on his books, even with the expenses that came up unexpectedly as they always do. Still there was machinery to be repaired, or at least maintained, over the winter in preparation for spring work on some fields, and harvest, following that in other fields. Though Julie had gotten most of the hinges welded onto the steel panels again that they needed for livestock; there were the grain bins and other jobs that would require time. In farming and ranching, it's always playing one hand against the other. He didn't mind making a mistake now and then. That was a part of life. He just tried to keep them to a minimum. That, was a part of good business.

He gazed through the windshield at the increasing precipitation. It had changed from sleet to snow. One-hundred-twenty miles to go. Warren, whom he had not seen since his college days, had both a farm and a dairy. Keeping in touch with his friend occasionally over the years, he knew that Warren's brother now had just bought his own farm, and that the cattle in his truck would help stock it. In exchange, he would receive the twenty thousand dollars, plus an old, small header used for harvesting. He would tow it back. He thought of Two-Jay, of Michaela, and Julie. He thought of their time together. Sometimes the work made their relationships more interesting and enjoyable. Sometimes it did the opposite. Michaela needed her own time with Missy regularly and that required privacy and quietness. Missy was not even taken outside when large machinery was being used. She was a competition horse, and reserved for that purpose, as free from disturbing influence as possible.

"She's a performance woman!" he said of Mickey, out loud in the cab of the dually truck, braking a little as it became more slick. He continued thinking about her and began to realize things he hadn't known about the woman he loved. A performance woman... he thought, then added. "She needs to be treated the same way. The right conditions, the right leading and the right time together." As another truck came from the other direction, he braked more than necessary for safety. Not only were the value of the trucks involved, but the living cargo. If there was an accident and he was moving slowly enough, maybe there wouldn't be any damage to the cattle.

At one hundred-ten miles toward his destination, at eight p.m. he stopped at an all-night truck stop. The temperature had dropped to twenty-eight degrees Fahrenheit. Checking the stock, the cattle had ridden with no problems, and the trailer, with vents mostly sealed against the cold, was sound as well. Having not risked an accident by using the phone while driving, he called Mickey now. He longed to hold her. Her phone rang first with no answer. Calling the house, she answered instead of Julie.

"Hello, Jack?"

"Hello Michaela...how are you?"

"We're making it here. The winter whipped in here all of a sudden and I have Missy wrapped like a mannequin." She sounded tired, even weary.

"No problems? How's Julie?"

"She's fine, but she is out looking for a lost calf. She counted them three times when they were huddled in the lee of the shelter. One is missing. I stayed here in case you called. I think she has a phone though."

"I miss you Mickey! Will you take care of yourself for me? Like I would take care of you? There is not another you in the world. There are four billion girls in the world, but only one you! I've been driving for fifty miles thinking about that." She had to admit, though he hadn't spoken like this before, he had been increasingly attentive, desiring to please her more acutely lately.

"I will, and you take care of you. I was thinking today about our first ride together. It was such a nice time. It makes me miss you." Silence returned as she waited. Finally, he spoke.

"I know, I think about those things too. Mick... um... Michaela...when you brush down Missy, think of me. When you talk to her, keep me there with you. When you are planning your goals with her, know that I support you and am there too. And if there is ever anything that you need me for...anything I don't know about, I'm here for you, no matter what."

"She realized that he had really been thinking about her. It wasn't merely silliness in dating like young kids. It wasn't whatever Jack would call it...um...just waxing rhapsodic, probably. She truly meant the world to him. And she knew that now. He must know more than she realized, to have included Missy and dreams in his thinking like he did.

"I'll remember Jack. I will! And Jack, I'm here for you too! Whenever you want me, okay?"

"Thank you, I know. It won't be long and I'll ask... you just think about what your answer will be, okay?" She smiled again at the tongue-in-cheek reference to the first days of their relationship.

"Okay, I'll think about it. I love you Jack."

"I love you Michaela. That won't ever change, it'll only grow stronger. You will be eighty one day, and I'll love you so much that you wouldn't even recognize me now." He had a way with words that cut right through her. He could actually *say*, what he meant. Most people couldn't.

"Jack, I um... thank you. Goodbye." The discussion lasted less than two minutes, but said everything. They might have spoken another half hour, but nothing could have been added to what they meant. What did he know? What had he found out that he would've mentioned brushing down Missy, or her dreams? How could he have found out what was on her mind?

174

Jack bought a coffee and crackers at the gas station. When he arrived back at the truck, the cab was still warm from the engine's idling. He put the truck in gear and slowly pulled out, onto the two lane highway. Heading north-northwest he found the highway signs without difficulty, but he kept thinking about Mickey. He had finally gone far enough in his thinking that while driving, he had actually tried to *find* things wrong with her. He had been brave enough to *look* for faults. After all, he had told her that he never wanted to settle for less than best in anything. There was nothing definite that came to mind. Maybe there would be after living with each other privately. In those times when you eat together, sleep together; have success together and trial together, maybe there would be something of a shortcoming in her. There was at least something in everyone else he knew, especially himself. He always found things about his work or attitudes or other things that could have been better. He could have had a number if women in town or in the county. But deep down, he knew that it would have been a train wreck. He knew most of them. And while some of the women in the area were good women, he just wasn't right for them, or the reverse. Mile after mile, he navigated slick roads and the increasing depth of snow. Once at a stop, he had to use four-wheel-drive to gain forward traction. Finishing the coffee and crackers, he slid into a mindset of wondering about the future as he drove. Mile after mile his mind wandered, to the good. Sometimes it wandered to the possibilities of life. He thought of Julie at the ranch. He also thought of Michaela's future as a rider in a demanding sport. He felt real pride for her.

Thirty miles to go before he reached Warren's farm, he wondered what Mickey had meant when she was speaking her thoughts out loud to Missy. What was it that she had meant? There was something distant about the whole thing. Mysterious or distant, he wasn't sure which. It was something he couldn't put his finger on just yet.

Delivering the cattle at one a. m. left no energy for anything, least of all hauling back the header on icy roads. Already sore from the tenseness of driving the rig under such conditions, he would sleep and begin back soon. He shouldn't have come. He should've had someone else haul the cattle there if he couldn't. But, that wasn't the way he used to doing things. At any rate, the eight head of cattle were delivered and he was paid. The check felt good in his pocket. As soon as the roads were better, he could leave for home. At ten a.m. the roads were reported to be passable.

With six hours sleep after small talk was deducted from his time at Warren's ranch, Jack started the engine. Planning, thinking and envisioning; the things that usually came easy to him, came difficult this morning. He could drive well enough, but that was it. Curious as to whether Julie had located the calf, he called.

"Hi Jack. Everything go okay?" Julie said flatly.

"All done. You okay sis? Did you get the calf?"

"Things are okay with the ranch, but the wolves got the calf, maybe coyotes, but they got him hard...looked like wolves, I'm not sure which. If I'd had my gun, they would have looked like the cat!" Jack became sullen. He hated to lose any stock. He felt a sense of failure, or at least shortcoming at the loss of an animal.

"You okay then? You didn't say about you."

Me? Yeah...I'm alright, I guess. But...well, Jack I think there is something wrong with Mickey. She's been in bed since last night and won't tell me what's wrong." Like a ship's fog horn blast penetrating ocean coastal clouds, her words cut .through his fuzzy head immediately.

"Michaela? Sick? What is it...do you know?" He remembered what she had just said. She had already answered that question. It was clear now to him that he wasn't fully alert.

"She's weak and quiet. That's all I know. I keep checking on her. At least I can be in her room part of the time. I'm checking on her Jack."

"Julie, take her to the doctor! I don't care what it takes! If it takes my half of the place to pay for it, you make sure that she's alright, you understand? Can you do that for me? Take her to the doctor and I'll be there in an hour and change. Go to Carson Hospital! Don't let her give you any excuses!"

"Jack, it may not be that serious. Don't be hysterical. Let's find out what it is first."

"NO! YOU TAKE HER! NOW! YOU DO IT! I'M TELLING YOU TO DO IT!" He yelled at Julie. He never yelled at her. The last time he had yelled at her was when they were ten years old. After half a minute, his tough and resilient sister replied flatly. "She doesn't want to go, Jack."

"Listen...YOU WANT ME..." he said, calming slightly, "to call one of the other places around there, Nelson's or McKinnet's farm, and get someone to come over and get her? TAKE HER NOW! I don't know what it is, but there is something we don't know." Julie was silent on the phone for seconds. It seemed like minutes.

"Okay Jack, I will. I'll get her there. See you soon." And in a moment, she was gone. He had some comfort, at least. There was one thing he knew. Julie was going to get her there. Nothing, absolutely nothing would stop Julie when she set her mind on something, least of all a sick woman. She had told him that she would get it done, and she would. Looking at a map he had kept handy, he planned a turn south at the next highway intersection to travel the fastest route to Carson.

Jack thought. He worked on what it could be. The whole distance there he thought about it. Recalling every bit of information, everything he knew about her, he added it together; working on it. He couldn't put it together into anything definite. He just didn't have enough information. Jackson Gentner sped fifteen miles-per-hour over the highway limit for as long as he could while hauling the long, heavy implement. He pushed the limit of safety until the header started swaying behind him, less controlled, and becoming dangerous. Clear headed enough to realize that it wouldn't help anything if he was in the hospital also, he backed off, trying to relax. Trusting Julie on something like this was easier than trusting anyone else would have been. She was tenacious once she had decided on a matter. The City of Carson, for him, one hour away, would still be there when he got there and so would they.

J J

Carson, a city nearly four times larger than Redlands, and where everyone traveled to for things you couldn't get at home, had become over time, an important place for the surrounding counties. The hospital was part of that general importance. There were no suits in Redlands, unless of course a person wore a western one for a rodeo, parade or other celebration. Here in a different atmosphere, Jack walked into the hospital in boots, jeans and a work shirt, still stained with work dirt and overnight sweat. He removed his ranch hat at a general desk inside the entryway.

"Excuse me, I'm looking for Michaela Hensley's room." He already had a dislike for calling her by her last name. He knew and she knew; the three of them all knew that she should have his name. And she would, as soon as he could arrange everything.

"Yes sir, she is on the second floor, in room seven." He left the desk, simply lifting a hand to wave in a friendly way at the receptionist. It was uncharacteristic of him not to say thank you, or some other basic, polite response. But now, in this minute, he found himself only focused on one thing. Jack took the stairs, not wanting to wait on the elevator. He skipped them three at a time, his boots barely missing getting caught on the last, arriving at the second floor. Jerking the door open with enough force that the nurses at the monitoring station down the hall heard the swish of air from the movement. He made his way to room seven and stopped. Entering slowly he looked to see if any nursing checks on her were in progress. They weren't. The lights were dim and she lay in front of him, appearing small and weak in that moment. Sleeping, he looked at her chart on the wall. IN PROGRESS, was all it said? There were procedures listed along with doctor's names beside each, but there was nothing he could discern. He leaned over her, wanting to kiss her. However not waking her, he kept back. She looked soft, even vulnerable. Ordinarily, on Missy or helping at the ranch, she looked strong and vibrant. She appeared weaker here, in the soft light of the hospital room. Though tired, he didn't think he was imagining her condition.

Moving back from her side, he stood up straight while focusing on the louvers in the windows which were now closed. He took a breath and turned slightly, toward the end of the bed. He saw Julie. She remained still, staring at him in the soft light. She half laid and half leaned on the end of the loveseat sized seat. Eyes open, she didn't rise, but just lifted one hand and gave a simple half-wave. Moving to her side, he touched her slightly on her shoulder. She didn't move. She lay there clearly awake, she just wasn't animated like he normally knew her. She motioned to him with a finger. He bent slowly as she whispered into his ear.

"You were right! She needed to be here! They haven't figured out the whole thing yet, but it's pretty serious." He looked Julie in the eyes. His tough, assertive Julie was missing. In her place a pensive woman with anxiety in her face. She carried a weight of concern, of love, for Mickey. She was looking to Jack for strength.

"Okay, thanks." He stood again, staring at Michaela. With an intravenous drip flowing and a preventative oxygen mask on, she seemed so different from the Mickey that roamed freely around the ranch and held such a bond with Missy. As he stepped away from the loveseat, his boot slid on the polished floor. Mickey heard it, waking. She focused her gaze in the semi-darkness. "Jack? Is that you?" He stepped to her side in one move.

"Hi honey. What are you doing in here? Missy's missing you!"

It was a stupid thing to say, but it had just come out. He gazed into her eyes longingly.

"Oh Jack, I won't be here long." Her voice started strong and faded to weaker speech, all occurring in the same sentence. "I'll be back quick... I... Just am kind of tired right now." He brushed her hair back over the pillow. She seemed to enjoy the gesture.

181

"Okay honey, you rest for now."

J J

"It's a type of auto-immune disease, like Lupus, but with some other characteristics added, and others missing." The doctor looked Jack in the eye, sincere and understanding. He waited for Jack to answer, giving him time to think.

"So..." Jack said, easing his way into the confusing medical diagnosis. "It's treatable then, right?" The doctor took a deep breath. "Yes and no. There are specialists who work on this one illness and although a lot of progress has been made, there are still peculiarities, occurrences which are non-standard. Again Jack tried to clarify the information.

"Living a normal life?" he questioned, not forming his words into a proper sentence. Again the doctor hesitated.

"She may have to periodically take it easy, but on most activities, I think so." So this then, appeared to be good news at least. Whatever she needed day to day, whatever she lacked, whatever she needed help with; he would ensure that she had it. Money, the ranch, all he had worked for, though still a strong part of him, was of a lesser value now. He would focus his strength, his resources, his finances, whatever it took; to overcome this weakness and anemia in her life. She would be strong again; that is, if he had a say in it.

J J

"Jack... Jack....Honey!" Michaela whispered. She nudged him on his shoulder.

"Jack, you need to get up." The nurse had pressed the latch on the door to her room, but stopped to speak with someone in the hall before entering. Asleep from long hours of work and a desire to be near her, he half laid on the upper part of her bed next to her head and shoulders with his lower half hanging off barely touching the floor.

"Sir...sir." The nurse spoke annoyingly. "Sir, you can't lay in the hospital bed with the patient." Though Mickey's voice hadn't awakened him, the loud, brash nurse did. He rose, with a stiff neck and back. He opened his eyes to see Mickey smiling at him, amused that he had tried to crawl in with her. Normally, he would have been embarrassed at the scene of being caught looking so ridiculous. But all he cared about was her. All he would ever care about... at least in linear terms, in the horizontal of this life, was she and Julie.

"Sir, you *have to* get up!" His senses gathering, he looked down as he stood up, leaning over Mickey.

"How do you feel, honey?" She smiled a more energetic smile than she had the night before.

"Better, better some." He smiled at the news from her. He smiled more from her comforting tone than from the words she spoke.

"Sir you will have to let me in to check her!" Jack waved off the intrusive nurse. "Just a minute," he said, turning back to Mickey.

"What do you need honey? Anything? Can I get you anything at all?" The nurse looked as if she were at the end of a long shift and didn't need anything interesting at the last minute to give her day character. She stood beside him, inching closer to the patient and to Jack.

"Nothing honey, nothing right now. Just let her check me, then we can talk." The same suggestion from the nurse had only earned his rebuke, but at Michaela's word, he reacted as if it were a command. He moved back quickly.

The overweight nurse wearing all blue, carried twice as much body fat as she should have for her five-foot-three inch frame. She began her hourly procedure to check Mickey, and found all in order. The next round of checks would be by a different nurse. Jack paced, peeking around her shoulder to ensure that she treated his woman as she should.

J J

"I'm sorry I didn't say anything about it Jack. I planned on it. I just could never find the right time. I'm very sorry... please forgive me. It's been pretty good lately, I haven't been too bad. It's just that I ran out of my medicine and I wasn't making enough to cover the cost. Really Jack, I'm very sorry. Will you forgive me? "He waved off the request for clemency.

"Nothing to forgive. It was a private thing and we weren't really as close then as we are now. If you have your medicine, you can make it alright? You seem to have done okay."

"Yes, I was...but then I was on my own for the last six years. My mother has a fixed income and I don't know where dad is right now. He works in the feed business. It's been my sister that has been helping me a little with the cost of the medicine. Jack and Julie listened to her in the hospital room. Julie, so capable at everything she put her hand to, had never in her life felt so helpless.

Mickey continued. "Missy is the only thing I have that is worth much, except my truck. I've been competing being sponsored by a breeding farm in Texas owned by friends of my family. It was a good arrangement, but I had to take this last year off and I came here to work with her because I couldn't stay where I was. And here I had access to a rented stable for Missy. My job at the elevator helped a lot." Jack looked at Julie who had obviously been thinking the same thing. He didn't even need to ask Julie if she supported the idea. He knew she would.

"We'll build a proper training round for her, or whatever it is that you call it. We'll build it at Two-Jay. And you can work her as much as you want. You can compete again as soon as you feel stronger. You can work with Missy every day if that's what you need to do."

"But I have to work my job. It helps with the cost of everything. My sister has a different arrangement now and... Well... I don't know."

"You're with us. If you want to work at the elevator when you are stronger, that's fine. But there really isn't a need to do that. We're doing okay." The news made her look tentatively happy. She wanted to say more, but couldn't. Clear to him that she was getting tired again, he waited. She began to cry. Then, in the rarest of moments, Julie came to her side and kissed her on the cheek. Don't worry about any of it. You're *my* sister too! And if my older brother can't handle keeping you in the shows or whatever else you need. You come to me. That's what sisters are for, you know?" Michaela, very tired, wept tears and put both arms around Julie and kissed her. "Thank you, thank you Julie." Her arms fell limp back to the bed. She fell asleep in seconds. Julie pulled the covers up to her chin as she looked at Jack, wondering what he really thought. They moved away from the bed.

"Jack..." Julie began, but fell quiet when Mickey raise an arm a few inches off the bed, awake again, to get his attention. In a single move he was at her side. "Jack...she whispered above the IV machine's soft whir. She waited, getting strength before continuing. The room was quiet and the three were close enough to touch one another.

"Jack... my Jack...do you... still...want me?"

Moving close to her, he sat on the bed. He leaned down to her, kissing her on the cheek and forehead. Hugging her as best he could in the position in which she was laying, he whispered to her softly.

"You are my heartbeat Michaela. Everything that I am or have has been saved for you." Julie couldn't hear his words. Too tired for conversation, Mickey began to cry again.

With one hand around four of his fingers, she hugged him in the only way she could.

"I'm so tired. But I love you Jack, more than anything. I love you both."

Surrender

"Mickey, can you make it into the kitchen? I'll make you breakfast if you would like that? If not, I could bring it to you." He spoke through the door to her room.

"Come in Jack, I'm always decent." He entered, hungry to see her.

"You look well. He said, honestly. You sure you can make it in there? I'll carry you if you want."

"Nonsense, I'm almost back to my old self again, honey. I've just been tired the last week, that's all."

Taking his hand, she smiled and seemed stable, but walked slower than she had in past months. She covered the distance of fifty feet from her room to the kitchen with little problem.

"Thank you for walking me Mr. Gentner. You are a gentleman." He bent to kiss her on the lips. It was a deep, sincere kiss; one that is shared when one person wholly belongs to another. He lifted her up slightly and kissed her on top of the head for good measure.

"I think you are doing great, filly."

Since she had been so weak, his affection for her had actually increased. Though he had always desired her, he had always made sure to give her enough of her own space. Now it was different. She appreciated and even desired the extra attention as they entered the warm, tile kitchen on a chilly morning. She sat as he made her an omelet and hash browns; his specialty.

"I'm doing pretty well, honey. Better every day. Once I get my strength back, then I can concentrate on the obligation to the hospital," she said.

"Obligation? he asked, as he stirred the pan.

"You know, the bill for being in the hospital. I signed a thing saying I'd pay two-hundred-dollars per month until it was paid. With my salary at the elevator, it will take a while. They volunteered to pay five hundred dollars of it. It's really nice of them, but it's still a lot. And Missy's expensive. I sure enjoy having her here. Even though it's not a proper training area we can simulate a lot of the movements and runs."

"Uhh-huh," was all Jack replied, trying merely to listen as he scrambled an egg and put a small amount of cereal into a bowl for her. On a second trip to the table brought enough milk in a cup to wet it.

"I'm relieved that you are better honey! I was really worried about you when I was driving."

"You don't have to say it. Julie told me all about how you were yelling at her to get me to a doctor when I didn't want to go. That must have been an interesting exchange of wills!" He flipped her eggs around in the pan. The western style, tan color backsplash behind the stove-top gleamed and reflected the eggs in the well-kept kitchen.

"Yeah, that is a good phrase for it! An exchange of wills, and I'll have you know, I won!"

"Yes! I know. Thank you, too. I could have really done myself in by not taking the medicine."

He sat her food down on a checkered placemat that lay in front of her, followed by the salt and pepper shakers. "Not taking your medicine?" he asked, honestly not knowing to what she was referring.

"It's true Jack. I thought I was going to be alright. I was feeling really good the last four months or so, you know? I just ran out, that's all. What with keeping Missy and the limited work I've had in the off season at the elevator, even with staying here I couldn't afford the cost of it so often. So I decided not to keep using it every day. I was taking it and everything, just not like I should have. Not very smart of me, but it's...pretty expensive." She ate a bite each of the omelet and potatoes. The cereal, she would eat after the rest. She would be crunching hungrily through it after

190

finishing the eggs. Thanks for breakfast! You know, you're not a bad cook." Jack sat with her, listening smiling while watching her.

"Michaela, is it that bad? I know you haven't been working as much, and I know the feed for Missy adds up. But you have to take them, you know." He saw a shadow of concern come over her face.

"I know, I will try, but this medicine is high. It's not like the less expensive stuff I used to take." He smiled a wide grin and kissing her forehead, he brushed her cheek with his finger.

"Don't you worry about it? You need it, and you'll have it!"

She kissed him. "Thank you Jack. That's nice. But before I can afford the medicine, I have to take care of the bill from the hospital. I mean, I can afford *some* of the meds... but..."

"Oh yeah, about that. I spoke with the hospital. We worked out a deal and it's been taken care of, as of yesterday."

A look of astonishment came across her face. The spoon fell into the bowl with a 'clink'.

"Jack! You paid it?" He shrugged. "Most of it I paid two days after we left the hospital. The rest was paid yesterday, so don't worry about it. Michaela, we three, you Julie and I are a family, already. Julie would tell you the same thing. We three will meet all challenges together. SO TAKE YOUR MEDICINE! "He said loudly in a mock yell at her.

She began to cry, not knowing what to say. He sat in front of her.

With a handsome face, clean shaven and a clean, light blue western shirt with pointed pocket flaps. His blue eyes were intensely kind as he looked at her with such appreciation for her as a woman and friend. Frustrated at her emotional state, she shook the napkin she used to wipe her eyes.

"I'm so darn emotional lately! Just a darn cry baby!"

"Your cereal is getting soggy. He said with a chuckle. "Plus, you are crying in it; that doesn't help" At that she began laughing. After kissing him a full, heart filling kiss, she ate the rest quickly, looking at him the whole time.

As he sat watching her, he found himself amused at her characteristics. He loved her more than ever as she sat in her pajamas with horse prints on them. This twenty-six year old woman looked a bit like a little girl as she ate the last of the cereal. He gave a small whistle as he ran a finger over the rough finish of the stone country table. When her eyes met his, he spoke, continuing the imaginary design with his finger.

"You know, I've got this girl see... and she's really quite something. I've made up my mind that I will marry her, but haven't asked her yet, you see?" She looked at him with an exaggerated animated amazement and anticipation.

"Yeeeaaahhh?" she said.

"Yep, so I've planned as a wedding present, since I know she'll say yes..." He put his hands up to his collars and tugged at them in a gesture of self appreciation. "...that I will let her redecorate a few of the rooms like she would like them. You know, to make the place more hers. What do you think? Is that a good idea for a country guy who's trying to do something special for his lifetime girl?"

She became still, her tongue running around her teeth inside her mouth. "Lifetime girl..." Mickey repeated. "Lifetime girl..." That meant more to her than redecorating or anything else he might ever give her.

"LIFETIME GIRL!" she said. "You call her that and she will like anything you do for her, I guarantee it!"

"Good! Well, since this girl is something really special, and you are a woman of vast insight," he said, waving his arm to the horizon. "I thought I'd get your opinion on that. I'm glad you agree with my ideas. It makes me feel optimistic that she will feel special and important." She stared at him, sitting together in the kitchen, in the quiet of the morning. She pulled her napkin to her face and looked away from him, crying again.

"Oh, Jack... that's so beautiful! I don't know what to say." He moved close across the table to her. "Well, just don't tell her, please. I want it to be a surprise."

"Okay," she sniffled. "I won't."

"I love you Michaela."

He was so sincere. It wasn't her illness, it wasn't being emotional, it was him. He melted her.

"Oh Jack, I love you so much! More than the whole world! And in a minute, I want to hug you like crazy, but right now, I really have to pee!" Laughing a wintertime, breakfast laugh together, he stood up to come around the table to her. His polished, solid silver belt buckle caught the morning sun shining through the window and flashed a sparkle of light around the spacious kitchen. He picked her up and carried her.

Stars

At ten-thirty-seven in the evening, the young, new moon had fallen below the western horizon. The mid-February chill of winter on the plains began reaching for any mammal still roaming about and not in their places of nurture. Sharing the cold with those creatures still mobile, Mickey looked up, standing underneath a canopy of stars and held her breath. Tens of thousands of stars, all colors and brightness's shone over her head like a garland around her from horizon to horizon. She gripped tight to Jack's hands as his arms wrapped around her, but she said nothing. There was nothing *to* say. There was nothing to add to what they felt here together. For ages of ages until now, men had looked up as the stars told their story. There was nothing that man could add to what the Creator had wrought. As her eyes, alight in the expanse, gazed upward; Jack held her from behind. They shared the immense quiet, and heard the heart rending beauty of the song of the stars. Balanced between them, there was just enough soul of mind and heart to be in union with the heavens.

In a reverent whisper, Jack quietly showed her the brighter stars and named them one by one. "Look, there is Sirius! It's the brightest star in the sky. And up a little, there is Rigel, the seventh brightest. There is Saiph, Bellatrix, and Betelgeuse, see how red-yellow it is?" She nodded respectfully without saying a word. She pulled his arms around her, tighter against the cold. But even without them she would have stayed.

"There is Mintaka, Alnitak and Alnilam. They're in one of the best known constellations in the sky." He brushed her cheek with his while telling her where to look next; as if they were standing in the library of the heavens and normal speaking would violate the sanctity of the experience.

"There is Aldebaran, the thirteenth brightest star. And above that and to the right, the Seven Sisters. They are called The Pleiades. They are one of the most beautiful star clusters that can be seen with the naked eye. And they are mentioned in many ancient texts, including the Bible! When you see them through a telescope and you look slightly to the side while viewing them, you can see the cloth of heaven." He whispered softly, giving to her a share of the experience he had enjoyed all his life. "There are clouds of dust and matter where stars form. Gravity pulls them together. Once they form, the stars shine within all the clouds they came from and make them shine too. See how the Pleiades are very blue in color?" Again she nodded. "They are newly formed stars and very hot." His respect for this experience awed her.

For two hours, long after their feet were numb in the twenty degree air, their hearts were alive and warm. Their minds were inspired beyond what can be understood in the light of day. A soul experience and a love experience; this more than any other moment they had enjoyed together brought him into her heart. What kind of man was he who had captured her? What kind of man was this that, although kind to his animals, still did good business; a man that could maintain his integrity in a world where simply keeping an extra dollar received in change by human error was so easy? This was a man who could name the stars on a quiet night together, to put light into the mind of the woman he loved. This was a man who had waited for the love of his life, rather than settled for immediate gratification. Michaela knew then, at that moment that no matter what else happened in her life she didn't want to be without Jack. There was no other man who would measure up to him. Anyone else would be a disappointment measured alongside him. In the last moments before they walked back to the truck, she held his arms around her. She looked up and beheld the glory of God in the seeds of nature. She didn't move, even though she felt the tear that had begun to slowly roll down her cheek. After mere seconds, it froze there. She deeply breathed in the night. Words would have ruined it.

Walking slowly back to the truck hand in hand, they remained silent. Letting her in first he shut the door behind her with a soft click. As they both sat quietly in the truck, still under the canopy of stars, they didn't move. Another half hour past as the stars overhead made their nightly progression to the west, telling the story of the constellations. Jack started the truck to warm it, but still said nothing. Fifteen minutes later he looked to Michaela as she looked upward through her window, within her own thoughts. She shivered slightly, then looked to him and nodded. He put the truck in gear to head home. From the field of grass, high above his farm, where they had spent their day of the picnic, they had stood and shared something no one else had that night. They hadn't yet been married and they hadn't yet made love. But they had been one. During the drive home, the entering of the house and the moving to their separate rooms for the night, not a word was spoken. Jack understood. He had been there by himself many times. Now he had shared it with a woman who could understand these things. No words had been necessary.

Changes

Offering to stay on at the Redlands elevator for one additional week, Mickey looking forward to being at Two-Jay full time, worked her job with flair. Cleaning, building a cheat sheet for the next person who became the elevator 'everything person.' At the week's end, she celebrated the changes both current and soon-to-be, in her life, by buying Jack a new pair of cowboy work boots. Not too expensive, but worth the money, she left them on his bed, for when he came in from the field. Domestication, something that she had desired, but put behind her while working hard, now came to the front of her thinking. She knew that whatever life held going forward, good or bad, it would be better experienced with Jack. He was a rare man. And as for herself, she liked to think that she had a lot to offer him and had saved the best of her for him. The thoughts of cooking and cleaning as a kind of service to another, had not taken front place in her thinking ever in her life. Even now, it was not that she desired to be subservient. But rather desiring to serve him, in love, with her whole dedication was something different. That would require at times, a different humility from that she had known when losing a competition. This was a kind that built someone else up. Something that would make another person greater that they would have been otherwise. It had come so rapidly to her! How would Jack explain it? Possibly as in some kind of chemical equation, the existing state of a substance was stable until another influence was added and the equation changed... something like that anyway. She was definitely experiencing changes. Julie, by herself, not to mention Jack, had been a great equation changer in her life. Julie made her laugh, cry, roll her eyes in exasperation, and even living the experience of her vicariously through Jack's reactions to her had enlarged Mickey's heart and experience in life. Her life had indeed become much larger. She desired not only to be the object of his affection, but to serve him in love; something definitely not seen much in society anymore. She could do that, and would.

Day to day Mickey realized that the work at Two-Jay would require her involvement. One day, if Julie found a man; no, *when* she found him, she might leave, making the necessity of learning Two-Jay even more urgent. Working with Missy, on their routine, keeping her in top form and staying sharp was taxing. While helping work the ranch and farm where she could, she had a realization. Brushing out Missy after a few exercises on the third Wednesday in March, she knew that the years of work, largely alone, with some sponsoring became great on her. It is something that she loved doing. But now it began falling under the heading of changes in her life. By Friday, her last day at work, she had realized she was becoming a woman who was content. It was such a strange experience being content. She had always strived, worked and pushed for some goal in life, in her week, her day. But now she was fulfilled for the time being. Maybe that would change in a month or six? Who would know that? Frequently thinking of the life and love experiences that she had gathered with Jack and Julie, it was like a new type of life. For five years, her world had consisted of work in preparation for competitions, or in maintaining the health and strength of a horse. Picking up money and a few support people where she could, it had already been a long road. Most of those training years she had spent with Missy, completing her as a competitor in a tough sport. Once she had made gains in her field, another challenge was holding them. Now with Missy at or nearly at her peak, she was content. It seemed so strange.

In a week or a month who knew what might happen? How long would it be before Jack would make their engagement official, she didn't know. One thing that she knew, was that Jack, had his own idea of what the *right time* would be. Until then, or after, she would keep at least part of her life in her own room at Two-Jay. "It's okay," she said to herself at the end of her last day working in town. She didn't need a firm date. She knew it would happen. And until it did, she couldn't be happier.

J J

The winds of March had come to the plains on cue with the first week of the month and had remained throughout it. Vaccinations, evaluating cattle, moving them to new pasture and disking the soil, were all things they worked together. Although Mickey knew much about livestock, there was a lot to what she needed to learn about intense farming. Now in the later part of March, some seasonal drilling was done. A little milo, cane and even some corn were drilled on sections of Two-Jay Ranch. Learning to drive a tractor in the precise way to drill seed into the soil, and make tight turns within sometimes limited space, were all things she practiced during the month. In between, when there weren't pressing activities that she could help with, she worked with Missy. The question of whether she would compete again was always on her mind. She hadn't resolved that question, but worked with Missy regularly as if she had.

Preparing sandwiches for the three of them, she had them ready for the time when Jack and Julie came in the side door whenever they were done with their work. She made a real test of it, to put her best effort into them. Though simple, being one of the first meals that she had made for them, it became important. Adding small bits of condiments or vegetables Mickey built up each sandwich, adding a dash of a sauce she had found recently to cap it off.

As she drove to the western edge of Two-Jay property an hour later to drop a bale of hay for the cattle, she checked the fence line. It had become clear to her that the time had come for a major change. Though doing remarkably well in her recovery

202

now, she couldn't honestly see herself competing for at least a year. She shook her head as she drove the ruts of the well-worn path through the field. She had made a decision.

♩ ♩

Michaela had left the sandwiches ready for lunch. She would continue to feed the livestock while Jack and Julie attended more pressing issues after they each ate. They came in together from working in the field. Jack kicked his boots off before entering, with Julie following him into the kitchen.

"My beautiful woman!" Jack said, giving Michaela a kiss on her temple. Julie watched as she bent over washing her hands in the oversized kitchen sink. "Okay you two, you better get a room soon!" she said, smiling. Jack looked at Mickey, who was also grinning widely. "Nothing would please me more than to get a room of our own for a week!" Jack laughed.

"Hmm..." Julie sighed into the sink. "Disgusting!" She made a face and pretended to throw-up. "My brother, getting his love on... uuugh." Immediately she winked in humor at Mickey, whom she now loved dearly. Julie, happy for both of them, couldn't help but press the situation as they sat to eat.

"Well, when you can get your big boy pants on, my brother; and ask her to marry you, you can get your room. Until then, my shotgun is loaded so no moving into the breeding barn until then, unless you want to end up like the cat...pass me the mustard

203

please; a sandwich, any sandwich, is no good without mustard."

Jack stared at his sister with amazement, shaking his head. For all of his life, Jack had marveled at his beautiful, talented sister's ability to move during discussions from an important, say a life changing thing like marriage to the mundane in one sentence. It was to her as if they were the same in importance. Marriage, mustard... they both began with the letter em. Maybe that was it.

"I have something I want to do for you two. But you won't know what it is until you get your boy stuff together Jack and pull up your pants." Julie said. Reaching for a turkey sandwich, she patted Mickey's arm, who restrained the effect of the humor that seemed lost on Julie. "As for you, I'll keep pushing him and soon enough he'll be over the cliff!" Jack watched Julie as she chewed a bite of the sandwich. His was head turning again. She had such a graceful way with thoughts and words...like a dump truck. Just back the big beast up and dump out a thought; that was his sister. Maybe this strange thing came from working the range together for so many years since they were kids. Maybe it was something else. He didn't know. Julie gave Mickey a slap on the shoulder on her way to the back of the house. The swinging back pockets of her well-proportioned work jeans made the woven pattern on the denim rise and fall with a style that was only hers.

Jack still sat, nibbling on the remains of a second sandwich. Mickey sat next to him as he finished it, seeming lost

204

in thought. She interrupted his contemplation.

"Jack, I have made a decision," she said, gathering his attention.

"You have? An important one?" He downed the last bite and finished his tea.

"Pretty important. I have decided to sell Missy."

It hit him like a brick. It would have made more sense to Jack if she had hit him on the foot with a hammer.

"Sell Missy? Michaela, you love her and you work with her. How are you going to do that? Why?"

With a sense of purpose and more security about a decision that he had ever seen in her, she explained. "She needs to compete Jack, she needs to work or she'll lose her edge. I am not up to the demands of competition right now and she is. Another thing; she is valuable. If she doesn't work, that value is going to decrease rapidly. If I sell her, I can use the money and help out around here and maybe for our future."

He had to admit, her reasons made sense. Even so, he remained quiet, thinking. At last he spoke.

"Honey, if you think that it is best, she is your horse. I will always remember her." At this, her eyes began to well with tears, even so, her resoluteness remained. "Oh Jack, I will miss her every day of my life! Always. But it's just the right thing to do."

Goodbyes

As Mickey walked into the Redlands Grain Elevator office one last time, she felt happy, yet melancholy. She had worked in the office, not quite seven months. But she felt close to the few others who worked there or managed for the owning grain company. She knew them. Though her official last day had been the previous week, she sat and visited with the owner and the few hands that were there; those who received, measured and delivered grain. A small cake and a card from them, atypical for the crusty crew, made the goodbye a truly *good* one. They knew of her tentative plans to marry Jackson Gentner, and were happy for both of them. Such is the closeness in a small community. A person knew people well. And although that carried difficulties with it sometimes, it also means that those in a community often took a large or small part in the celebrations of each other during their lifetimes. Also people often feel the loss more when a person in a small community dies. For Mickey, and Jack, a card would be sent to Two-Jay ranch upon their marriage, and a number of the men in town would buy him lunch or shake his hand in their strong grip when passing on the street. It is and would continue to be a good life together.

J J

Walking through the front door of the house, Mickey listened. "Anyone here?" she called. No one called in return. Julie was likely working on the livestock and Jack on machinery, if he wasn't disking. She wasn't sure he would be however since it had rained recently and disking wet soil often makes for more work later. Jack was not a do something twice kind of guy. She loved him for that. Setting the cake and card on the kitchen table, she walked back to his room. Looking in, she saw the boots she had bought for him out of the box and on top of the dresser standing neatly together. Curious, she wondered if they were the wrong size. She would remember to ask him later. She looked around his bedroom. She examined the way he kept his things. It was an insight. Most things were neatly ordered, though there were one pair of work jeans laying over a chair. Mickey walked around the walls of his room, looking at his memories. An award for calf roping hung on the wall. Memories from Two-Jay showed his parents and family where they were evident in pictures. As she stepped carefully around his things, she found a small stack of pictures of her and Missy printed on paper. She and Missy working together in various parts of their routine, were on most of them. They were carefully composed and beautiful photographs. She never knew that he had taken them. Not able to determine when he had taken them, she placed them back where they had sat. Looking out his bedroom window onto the hills several miles behind the ranch, she remembered good days. They were warming thoughts now as she realized how many good days they already had experienced together.

The wind blowing, as it does in March on the plains, made the window vibrate slightly. Looking down as she stood over his dresser, Michaela ran a finger across the top of it, trying to feel the man she loved. In an impulsive moment, she decided to snoop. No one was there. She had never looked in his dresser at his shirts or underwear and considering it lovingly humorous, she opened one drawer. Lightly touching his clothes in the drawer, she appreciated again the moments and blessings of her life. Lifting a pile of dress socks, which she had never seen him wear, she felt a solid box no larger than the palm of her hand. She pushed the drawer closed, stood still and then re-opened it. Instinctively she looked behind her back at the doorway, as she reached into the sock drawer. She pulled out the box. A label had been printed and was stuck to the top of a jewelry box. Michaela Gentner-Ring Sizing. He had already picked a ring and had it sized. How did he know her ring size? She couldn't figure it out. Opening the box she breathed deep. In a white gold horseshoe setting lay a series of small diamonds. Within the interior of the horseshoe was a yellow gold center, with a number one inscribed. She couldn't believe it. She would never have thought of a ring like that. It was beautiful in every way. Lifting it out quietly even respectfully, she slipped it on her finger. It fit. How had he known? Mickey turned over the ring after removing it. Over and over she examined it. When she read a short inscription on the inside of the band, tears welled in her eyes. It simply said; STARS.

As the door to the front of the house suddenly burst open, she heard the unmistakable voice of Julie speaking. She returned the ring and closed the box, slipping it back into his drawer, sliding it closed quietly. As she stepped into the hallway from Jack's room, Julie stepped into the hall from the front entryway. They startled each other, jumping back. Mickey, alert and thinking, spoke quickly. "Hi Julie! Say, do you know if Jack has tried the boots on that I got him a few weeks ago? They are in there, but they don't look worn." It was a nice save from an embarrassing situation. Julie walking like a woman on a mission, replied pleasantly but hurriedly.

"Oh, hey babe... I am in a run! I don't know if he did. You might try asking him when you are smooching with him in the hayloft or something. I have to grab my gloves and its back to the field." Mickey had come to enjoy it when Julie would launch off with something off the cuff, like that.

"Need help out there? I was going to pick up some groceries for us, but if you need help?" Julie came from her room with work gloves in hand, stopping to consider. "I don't know why I would've left them in there! What's that? Help? Uhh... Actually yes, I could use some help."

"Just let me put my boots on, and I'll be with you Julie."

"Take your time chickie, I've got to cop a squat in the little girls room anyway," she said, half closing the bathroom door.

They spoke in the truck as Julie drove. Heading to the south-west corner of Two-Jay, Julie began fishing for new information from Mickey as she tapped the steering wheel for the ten minute ride. "So... you getting excited Mick? Has that bum of a brother of mine does the honorable thing yet?" Mickey laughed audibly..

"For heaven's sake Julie, we're not meeting behind the barn to hide something, what a question!"

"Oh, I know... and you won't be at this rate! I don't know what's holding him up. He's older than I am but sometimes, I wonder, you know?" Again Mickey smiled, realizing she possibly knew something that Julie didn't. "Well, you know Jack, he's a thinker. He's probably thinking about the perfect time to ask, or whatever." Julie looked over at her sister in spirit, if not by marriage. "He could be, I guess. More than likely... he thinks that marriage is a lot like what we three have got, everyone in a separate room! Honestly, I can't believe he hasn't made a move on you yet!" Mickey's expression changed slightly, to one of introspective thought...

"Maybe he has," she joked. Now it was Julie who had to reason it out.

"Yeah... yeah... if that were true, I guess I wouldn't want

anyone knowing about it either. Jack! THE BIG LOVER! Yuck!" Julie said flatly, while looking over at Mickey winking. Mickey met her gaze and readied words on her lips.

"Jack is actually very romantic. But I think it's a side no one sees."

At that moment, Julie hit a hole in the dirt rut and bit her lip as she was looking at Mickey. It shook the pick-up. "I'll take your word for it. And I'm glad I don't see it. I mean, I'm told he's handsome, but he just looks like plain old brother Jack, to me! Yuck!"

Mickey told Julie of her first date with her brother, and how the waitress gave such a glowing view of him.

"Oh, that must be Jenny. She's alright, I guess. I'm glad Jack didn't get up with her or someone like her. There just aren't many women around here who are Jack's equal. He's very good at what he does, you know? And, I guess he is smart, always reading like he does."

"Yes, he sure is," Mickey agreed. With firsthand knowledge, she would always know him.

"Jack is a still-waters-run-deep, kind of person."

Julie mumbled to herself as she stopped the truck and got out. Mickey only heard part of it. But Julie could be heard grudgingly admitting that Jack was a good man. She was still speaking after she inspected a fence gate. As she climbed back into the truck she continued, still speaking. "... and that's why I still wonder about sweet ole Jack. Maggie Pearson thought she had her hooks in him, like a side of cold beef. But he couldn't talk to her, you know? Pretty, and she had good grades in school, he just couldn't talk to her. Jack's kind of a dreamer. And when he speaks, he needs someone who understands, you know what I mean?" Julie said, in a rare moment of shared insight.

"I do," Mickey said.

They pulled up to a small barn that stored some cattle supplement and salt blocks. The two of them loaded the eighty pound bags into the truck. Mickey put four of the five pound salt blocks in and slid them next to the supplement. Julie was still in a frame of mind, like a child trying to understand her world, but having to work at it. "I guess the man is okay, I'm glad he didn't get stuck with any dead weight for a wife." He seems to be doing okay on the dairy investment."

"Yeah, that worked out pretty well so far," Mickey added. Suddenly Julie stopped and leaned on the side of the truck, her head down, breathing deeply. "I'm glad he's got you Mickey, really I am. I make a lot of noise, but Jack needs you. I've known him for twenty eight years and he is a different man around you. You bring out the good in each other, I think. If I were to ever find a man in this world, which isn't likely, I couldn't deal with a wimpy little wing nut, rag doll! I'd smash him in the head or in the nuts for sure!" Mickey didn't look away as Julie spoke, but rather right at her. Julie remained mysteriously overt to her. Mickey thought her funny as well as insightful. "I'd really like a man," Julie continued, opening up in a rare bout of sister talk. "But I'm twenty-eight and haven't had any takers yet... I... Just don't know if I will."

After speaking, Julie stood quietly for two minutes looking at the land and listening for the cattle. Finally she banged her hand on the side of the truck. "Take care of him Mickey, in all areas of life. Take care of him huh? Real love is a rare thing... around here anyway."

♪ ♪

The truck and trailer came at eight-twenty in the morning on this Friday in late March. But Mickey had known about it for a week. It hadn't made it any easier. After an inspection of the horse by two men, and a very short demonstration of what Missy was capable of in performance, payment was made. Michaela walked the strong, award winning horse, her friend and companion, out of the corral and to the truck. Missy's hair on her mane was braided tightly and the light mane stood out in a bold contrast to the chestnut color of her body. She looked as nice as she ever had. She had been groomed and the two of them had said their goodbyes. Mickey cried privately the whole time. None of the preparation had made it any easier. She had gotten a good price for her friend, with whom she had shared competition victories. But that itself, had come at an emotional price. For two days Mickey said nearly nothing. She had known it was the right thing to do, but she had sold her friend and team mate. She had sold a part of herself...forever. She tried to think clearly about it all. *'It's the tough decisions in life that make you who you are.'* Jack had said that.

Mickey sat at the kitchen table finishing her coffee two days after Missy had gone, Jack strode into the room followed shortly by Juliana. Both of them knew that Mickey needed something. Not knowing what, but she needed something.

"Got the tractors and drills ready for the new fields Jack? Julie asked, pouring her coffee. "Everything is done, finally. Sorry I've been so out of pocket the last ten days ladies. I felt we had to be ready."

Julie turned from the tile counter of the large, western style kitchen that held the coffee pot and swung a leg over the back of a chair and sat at the stone table. She sat, sipping her cup without saying anything for a full minute. As usual, she was the one you wanted if it were necessary to give things an obvious push.

"Jack, I uh... I'm not rushing things at all. I mean it's your business, but I wondered if you had an idea when you were going to convince this girl here to marry you and set a date?" She removed the lid from a glass jar that stood on the kitchen table and took out a wafer cookie, broke it and nibbled on it while leaning on her elbows, staring at him. She then lifted her coffee to her lips as the silence remained. Jack looked at her. He decided that she was trying to ask a sincere question and not simply trying to be a pain. He answered the best he could.

"As soon as Michaela feels like talking about it," he said. He removed a plate from the refrigerator and warmed scrambled eggs in the microwave that he had cooked the night before. Another minute passed as he peppered his plate and downed the eggs.

"I'm okay guys," Mickey said. "I have just still been saying my goodbyes, that's all. She and I were a team. I'm just missing a team mate right now, that's all." Julie looked at Jack in silence over the end of a cookie. "But I am ready to help you two with whatever you need," Mickey continued. "And Jack, I'm ready to talk about *that* subject anytime." Jack looked at her and nodded as he turned to put his plate in the sink. He washed the dish and left the kitchen without so much as an additional word.

Five minutes later, he was dressed for driving into town, or wherever he planned to go. Julie had stayed with Michaela, though neither had said much. Jack's presence in the kitchen always made him appear to stand tall, in more ways than the physical. He was in control of the situation, always... he just kept a lot to himself.

"Mickey if you can help with the house today, Julie and I will be back shortly, I hope. I need her to run into town with me to have some things done to your truck. We'll be taking your truck. But I've left the house a little dirty."

"Yeah, hauling Missy around, my maintenance has gotten a little behind. I had already started picking up parts of the house.

I will keep going while you two are gone this morning." Jack came to her and looking her in the eye, smiled a warming smile. He kissed her on the forehead. "Soon honey...real soon." He followed up with kissing her on the lips and an understanding touch. Even a pinch on the butt. Watching them, Julie coughed into life.

"I think I'll need another cup of coffee to deal with all this affection. I've got to clean out the pens when we get back today, and I need a bracer!"

After they left, Mickey got into gear. She had wallowed enough. Soon... he had said; real soon. If there was anything that could lift her from missing Missy, it would be to be officially engaged to Jack. It would be something the whole town would know about and she could wear her pride in a way she hadn't been able to before. Besides the obvious though, she couldn't determine what 'real soon' meant. She thrust herself into cleaning the house. It would soon be her house, for real. She was more like Julie than she had ever thought. Maybe communication and the way the two of them expressed ideas were a lot different, and maybe Mickey had learned the fine art of horsemanship in a way that Julie hadn't. But she was still a lot more like Julie that she'd realized. She longed for love, and companionship in a way that she had always had difficulty in communicating. Standing at one end of the house and staring into the large living room, she threw herself into cleaning with a fierceness that was all her own. She wouldn't stop until she was done.

J J

"What do you think Julie?" Jack asked, as they examined the young horse. Julie looked at the American Quarter horse critically. Beautiful as she was, the sorrel coat fit the horse well and made her very appealing. A well-bred Quarter Horse, she stood slightly taller at the withers than Missy had as a horse bred for competition in equitation. At just under four years old, this horse was young, and only recently trained for riding, but by all accounts a fine animal. With the breeder present, Jack stood next to her, getting to know her.

"Fifteen-and-a-half hands Jack, and every bit a winner!" The man whom Julie had not met before, was confident in what he was selling. After saddling her, Jack mounted the saddle and simply sat, watching the horse's reactions to movements he made, and sounds. Leaning forward, almost stretching, he ran his hand back toward himself from the neck toward the withers and stopped with a pat. He moved in ways that the horse may have not experienced every day during his acclamation to riding. With a modest nudge, he moved the beautiful animal into motion, walking slowly around the grounds of the breeder's property. After fifteen minutes he drew her to a stop and remained standing. Another nudge and within a few lengths of the horse, had her at a trot. In his eye, the horse performed beautifully. Clearly a fine example of the capability of the breeder and trainer. The man, a friend had been a help in finding Mickey a horse of her own for the ranch. Walking the sorrel again for a few minutes, Jack brought her back to Julie, who had gauged and judged every move they had made from a distance.

"Julie, I think she's fine. Why don't you take her?"

Julie stood by the horse stroking her on her side and made a slow, long stroke from the throat latch outward; partly for the horse to get to know her, and part to feel the coat and sinew of her. She ran her hand down the shoulder of the sorrel and traced the leg down to the hoof, looking downward. She bent and felt the cannon of the lower leg. Still squatting, she looked over the horse from a low viewpoint. She patted the lower barrel, around the ribs of the relaxed animal. "Pretty fine Jack! I like her." Julie stepped into the saddle. For ten minutes, she repeated most of what Jack had done with the horse, becoming solidly impressed with her capabilities and health.

After the two men had a long talk about her and his breeding methods, Jack felt good about it, preferring the sorrel to others he'd seen. Jack had expressed his interest a month before in finding a ranch horse for Mickey. He had desired one that could also be a good companion for her as she lived at the ranch day to day. This animal seemed to fit the bill.

With the fee paid and the horse in the trailer, they started toward Two-Jay. Coming back into town from the north, they stopped for lunch at the steakhouse, parking the truck and trailer on the side street of the building.

"Good thing you got the tires on this truck, they were pretty bad." Julie said. Jack following her thoughts, nodded in agreement. Once in the door, and they had sat down at a table, they spoke honestly. Julie's reactions showed her to be more thought possessed than he had noticed lately. She joked with him, sharing the excitement of giving the horse to Mickey as an engagement gift.

"I knew you had something going Jack. To be sitting on your...um duff like you have, with Mickey wishing to be engaged and all. I knew it was something." Satisfaction showed on his face. "I've been looking for a while, I just hadn't found one that would be good for her," Then he smiled a natural smile, a real, true genuine smile that she hadn't seen in a while. Not a charmer smile, a little boy Jack smile; one that she remembered from childhood when he was really happy about something.

"I'm really happy for you two Jack. Or... I will be when you finally make a move!" She picked up her dinner fork and jabbed his arm for emphasis. Over her lifetime, he had come to love her abrasive but amiable ways, even if they were an irritation once in a while. He looked out the window still smiling, then back to her. In her faded work jeans with the large belt buckle displaying two jays side by side, and the thick sweat shirt she had worn for the morning chill, she was a handsome girl. He waited until she looked him in the eye. When she did he came at her confident and clear. "It'll happen for you too Julie, it will!" She looked appreciative. "Yeah maybe, who knows?" She shrugged. When their food was brought to them, it was brought by Jenny instead of the waitress who had taken their order. Always herself, she greeted them.

"Oh Jack! How ya been? Hi Julie! How are you girl?"

Julie lifted a casual right hand off the table and moved it in a wide arc of greeting. She managed a tilted head smile as she leaned on her left hand.

"Hi Jenny."

The waitress dropped her order pad to her waist as she stared at Jack sitting in his work shirt, and ball cap. He lifted his head and looked up at her. Her bowl haircut had gotten longer, now almost to her shoulders.

"Oh you two! I just can't believe it. Did you run out of girls latey, Jack? I mean, having to bring Julie in here with you like this? A twitch showed on Julie's face. Jenny oblivious, leaned over to Julie and spoke more softy, but loud enough for him to hear.

"Thanks for bringing him in Julie, we just dream about Jack! I miss him when he doesn't come in." And with that, she hurried away, happy in her day. Julie picked up a napkin and folded it. And with a mock attitude, put it in both hands. She turned it on.

"Oh that Jack and Jenny! Aren't they just the most! And he's just A-dor-E-ble!" Jack watched her animated act with a small smile. She threw the napkin on the table, stared at him for a second, and picking up the fork, jabbed his arm with it again.

"You are disgusting, my adorible brother!"

Looking down at her steak, she continued. "Where's the ketchup? Why would she bring a steak and no ketchup?" Jack still watched her, remembering their childhood. In spite of everything for all these years, he loved her. She was quite a woman. It had become quite a satisfying thing to have come so far together with her. Everyone knew Jenny, and everyone knew Julie. It's life together in Redlands.

"YO! Jenny! Ketchup over here when you can, babe!"

Home

Arriving back at Two-Jay four hours after they had left, the trailer rattled over the long driveway which crossed the front of the property. With the unnamed horse behind them, Jack put on the brakes and slowed as they saw Mickey at the front of the house. When viewed from the road, the left half of the front facade of the ranch style house looked clean and new. The three Bradford pear trees which had blossomed in the recent spring warmth, added to the effect of the fresh look of the facade. From where she stood in the front yard, the wall to the other end looked dingy by comparison. When they got close, it was clear that she had been power washing the front of the house. It had needed it. The dust, the storms, dryness and heat, had all made a difference over time. They drove past her around the curve toward the barn and corral. The spray, strong as it was, carried to the drive and coated the windshield of the truck with water. She smiled as she saw them go by, the windshield wipers coming on as they passed.

Twenty minutes later, they walked up to her. Jack smiled. "When I asked for help cleaning the house honey, I meant pick up a few things inside and put them away, not CLEAN THE HOUSE!" He shook his head smiling, even laughing. Julie stood with him with a sharp eye, like always.

"Looks good Mickey! Really good!" Julie said. "We should have done this a few years ago, Jack." Viewing the house from any angle, it looked better.

"I agree. Mickey if you want to take a break we can have lunch?" Jack said.

"Thanks, but I think I'll finish the front here and then eat." She answered energetically.

"Well!" Julie slapped her sides. "I will make us all something to eat and you two finish what you have to do before lunch." As she walked toward the back of the house, Jack moved close and kissed Mickey, dirty as she was and covered in wet clothes.

"You look nice! Even when you are covered in dirt! I've never thought of you in a dirty way before, but..." He put out his lip, pretending to think. It has possibilities." Mickey shook her head. Remembering all that Julie had told her about handling her brother, she reflexed, moving away and sprayed him with the power washer, soaking his clothes.

"What? What was that for?" he asked, shaking off water. She snuggled up close and kissed him solidly on the mouth, lingering, teasing.

"I've been talking to Julie recently about how to handle you! That's what you get when you talk dirty to me!"

It had to be! Jack sighed and nodded. "I see!" he said, as he stood dripping. "Well, if I am going to get this kind of treatment, I may as well go in and get it from her! I don't feel as bad about ignoring her, as I do ignoring you." He smiled and kissed her. Entering the kitchen, he was still wringing out the legs of his jeans. Julie noticed, curious. When he saw her examining him, he made his statement. "I see you have been contaminating Mickey!"

"What? What does that mean?"

I made an innocent remark and she hit me with the power washer!" Julie nodded approvingly. "Smart girl, she's learning."

♩ ♩

At eight in the evening, Jack sat at his desk, quietly studying the ranch's finances. Mickey came in, flopping on the heavy armchair near him.

"Tired? he asked."

"Yes! I have been working all day! It feels good though, to get a lot done."

"Hmm... serves you right for listening to Julie."

She stood up from the chair, came over to him, and putting her arms around him, kissed his neck. "Julie, is a very wise woman." She whispered, hugging him again. He looked her in the eye ensuring that she wasn't sick again as he made a face. She left him to his work, and walked back to her room as she heard his reply, calling after her.

"Sure! And then there's the one about the Three Bears."

Waiting until she was out of sight, he laid the bills that he held in his hand down on the desk. Opening the desk, he retrieved a small box, containing her ring. As he examined the ring, he thought. Popping the ring in the box, and the box back in his desk, Jack walked silently across the house at nine p.m. to the bath in his bedroom and took a long shower.

Sleep was good, for everyone. Jack woke up early on Saturday at five, before the sun. That much was normal for him. But he spent the next hour in the barn gazing at the horse that would be hers. The beautiful sorrel color of the American Quarter Horse appeared rich and deep in the incandescent lamps of the stable. The beautiful female didn't even have a name. She would soon. For better or worse, she would have a name...today, he guessed. He walked back to the house and into the kitchen, thinking everything over in his mind, planning this once in a lifetime event. Julie was there, cooking beef and eggs with cereal already set on the table.

"You gonna' ask her today?"

"Yes, in a half hour, I think," he said, as he stood by the rock table in the center of their kitchen. Julie set down the spatula she held and adjusted the burner downward. She came to his side, sliding up next to him. She hugged him. It was a real, genuine affectionate hug. The most real one in years.

"I love you Jack. I'm really glad I got to be part of this. Thank you." He put a long arm around his sister, six years younger than himself. He held her close for minutes, only the two of them in the western style kitchen. "We have shared a lot, huh sis?"

"A lot!" she said. It was all she said. Julie patted his lean stomach. "I need to check the food brother bear."

"Smells good, thanks for cooking. I'm going to wake her now. Be ready, okay? As soon as you call for breakfast, we'll come."

"Gotcha," came the soft reply through a sniffle.

Jack walked to Michaela's room. Listening, he heard nothing. Carefully turning the handle and inching the door open, she lay covered, asleep. Smiling his best, most convincing smile, he walked to the bed quietly, and touched her gently.

"Michaela? Michaela?" he said with increasing volume to his voice. The third try did it.

"Michaela?" he said as he gripped her shoulder firmer. She stirred.

"Wha... Oh Jack," she smiled fully, blinking in the semi-darkness; as if she had wished him to come wake her from a life she had spent looking for him. He kissed her gently and communicated to her through his gripping of her hand, that he had a purpose in waking her.

"Honey," he didn't even get out his words. She sat up in bed, wiping her sleepy eyes and hugged him with a grip more fit for a horse. Her eyebrows went up and she looked expectant, even though she wasn't sure what he wanted in her room at six-fifteen in the morning.

"Honey, come with me. I want to take you outside." Now she was confused. She had half expected something unusual over the next weeks, but outside? In pajamas at six in the morning? Outside? She pulled back the comforter and sheets. In her pajamas, she sat up.

"Okay... now? Where are we going?"

"Just come with me."

"Let me get my clothes on."

He had waited long enough however; they all had. Too long! He was ready and he wasn't waiting any longer.

"Now, please. Just come in your pajamas." Confusing her even more, she stood up.

"Okay, where's my shoes?"

He sighed. He looked at her and shook his head.

"Hmm," he said, picking her up in his arms as she held onto him. Just then, Julie called from the kitchen. "Breakfast is on...

get it or lose it, chumps!"

Jack held Mickey close to him. He carried her down the hall, swinging her as needed to navigate doorways and obstacles. Reaching the kitchen, Julie was gone, and the food was gone. He took long strides to the door and threw it open with her clinging around his neck. He walked the hundred foot distance to the barn in fifteen seconds. The door was open as he walked in. Mickey, completely confused simply clung to him.

"I wanted to talk, but wanted to be private," he said, as he sat her on the lower railing of a small stall for shorter livestock, such as sheep. She held to a corner post as she found her footing on the rail below her. Balancing, she waited as he stood in front of her. There, in the barn she sat at six-thirty in the morning. Fuzzy headed in the quietness, she sat next to Reacher who enjoyed sniffing her hair. Jack kissed her again. And pulling out the box from his pocket, he gave it to her. She understood immediately, hugging him in response. Not even opening it, Mickey couldn't let go of him. Finally he had to speak.

"Michaela..." She didn't respond. She didn't want to respond. He waited, allowing her to enjoy this moment in whatever way she wished. When she moved slightly, He took the initiative.

"Mickey, you're cramping my plans here," he joked. She smiled, but backed off to remain on the railing. He motioned to her to open the box. Complying without taking her gaze from him, she beamed. And looking down, she saw the ring as she had seen it before. Surprised then, now thrilled! She already knew what the inscription said. She simply slid the ring on her finger. The quietness of the barn was unique, except for Reacher sniffing her neck and pajamas. Thinking that he might warrant some oats this early in the morning, he waited at the ready. It made for a perfect atmosphere. Kissing her, he pressed the question home.

"Well?" he asked. She straightened on the railing, now fully awake.

"Excuse me, but I don't believe I heard the question," she said.

"Hmmm... I can see Julie's influence on you. Okay, Prissy Jams; are you going to marry me? Or am I standing out in a barn by a hungry horse at six a. m., looking stupid for nothing?"

"Oh Jack! Yes...yes, YES! Thank you for loving me! I love you so much Jack!" Two more minutes of hugs and kisses past until, figuring that the thing had run its course, he decided he could take the next step. He picked her up and held her in his arms. He suddenly looked at her, a little surprised, realizing from holding her that she wore nothing underneath the pajamas.

"Hmmm..." he said contemplatively. "I didn't know that you don't wear underwear to bed. She jabbed him in the shoulder as she held on to him.

"There's a lot of things that you don't know mister, YET!"

He looked at her smiling. He was contented. Her engangement had come off well. And she had been all that he had searched for in a woman and a wife all his adult years. He slapped her hard on her butt which sounded a loud 'smack' in the quiet air. Carrying her across the barn to the last horse stall. She held onto him with eyes closed, relishing her moment of joy that she had already determined would only come once in her life. When she opened them and focused, as she saw the stunning sorrel in front of her. She knew the horses that were kept at Two-Jay, she knew each one of them well. This wasn't one. She pushed back from him, looking him in the face, questioning him without speaking.

"She's yours Michaela. That is, if you want her. Julie and I thought that you would like a ranch horse of your own. And she's a nice one honey, kind of special."

Surprise, shock and admiration for the lovely animal in front of her shown on her face. She moved to get down from his arms. Jack restrained her, holding her tightly. "There is one more thing," he said.

"What else could there be?" she asked, looking at him, stunned by it all. "Your beauty here doesn't have a name. And, it was Julie who bought her for you... as a wedding gift!"

Speechless, Mickey said nothing. Still and in shock, she stood now, bare feet in the dirt of the barn. She had handled livestock and stood as an accomplished rider, yet she had never expected this.

"Julie? She...really?" He nodded and stared down at her feet in the dust. The dirt and hay of the barn floor, lay over her toes.

She threw the low barrier open deliberately, but slowly. She reached out gently to the handsome mare in front of her.

"Oh, sweetie..." Mickey said, as she began crying. She couldn't help it. "Oh sweetie, you are so wonderful. We will get along great! You are beautiful." Then, as if it dawned on her again, she stopped. "Julie! Where is she? Where is Julie? I want to thank her. I'll be right back." She turned to go out the stall and ran into Julie, smiling behind her and wiping a few tears of her own. They hugged each other as sisters and friends, in a way like never before.

"Oh Julie, thank you! Thank you so much! She's wonderful!"

"Nothing for you sister! All I'll ever ask of you is just one thing!" Mickey hugged her again, as Julie's belt buckle scratched her stomach through the thin pajama material.

"Anything... What?" She looked in the older woman's eyes.

"Just keep this no-good bum of a brother of mine here, out of my kitchen and out of my hair! Can you do that? Because I like you a lot, sis! And I don't want you to wake up one day and find him stretched out dead or anything. Okay?"

"Oh, Julie! Done deal!" And the two hugged again, Mickey in pajama's barefoot in the barn; and Julie with jeans and boots with an untucked tee-shirt. Mickey replied quietly and whispered in Julie's ear. "And I think I have just the thing to keep him out of your kitchen!" Her eyes glowed, full of anticipation for the future. Julie smiled. "I *know* you do honey. Welcome home!"

"Mickey stood alone in the barn stall with the beautiful sorrel. She couldn't or wouldn't think of a name yet. This was a special horse. In all likelihood, as special as Missy. She could tell that much. This horse *was* special. She leaned into the mare, her ear on the horse below the withers. They would have to ride together, they would have to talk, before she could decide on a name. For now, they would just be friends.

As Julie pulled the food out of the oven, having kept it warm while they were all in the barn. She spread it out on three plates; beef, eggs and some cantaloupe, still out of season, but worth the extra for this special day in early April. Mickey came into the kitchen from her room wearing jeans, a cowgirl shirt tucked in, and her ring. Proudly wearing the ring, she got out glasses and cups, pouring juice and coffee. Julie spoke to her nearly an hour after they had been in the barn together celebrating.

"Dressed already? Got underwear on?" she joked. Jack looked up from the newspaper at Julie. "How's that again?"

"Girl thing, brother... go back to nowhere land." The sisters laughed as Julie waved off the question by Jack. As they each ate slowly this morning, the multi-spot mini lights of the kitchen made her ring sparkle even more than it did normally. Mickey was beside herself. An engagement and new horse BOTH! A wonderful, new horse. All in one day! It was almost too much. As they ate, Mickey was almost giddy. It was to be expected. To make sure she wasn't unappreciative, she volunteered to do dishes.

"Forget that skinny butt!" Julie said flatly. "You go talk to no-name. And take her for a ride if you want...take the day off! If you don't like that extra saddle in the barn, you can use mine."

Michaela had always loved Two-Jay and the two of them. But now, today; she felt like a new woman. Although they had not set a date, at least their engagement was official. She walked up to her horse, again taken by her beauty. Julie had bought this fine animal for her. She still couldn't believe it. She cinched the strap, and put the bit in, all the time admiring her. Still in the habit of leading the horse in her trained style, she took no-name, as Julie called her, out into the spring sunlight. Speaking to her gently, trying to elicit trust in the beginning hours, she pulled on the saddle horn lightly and gave her other signals that her new owner was going to take her for her first journey together. When she felt the moment was right, she put her left boot through the stirrup, grabbed the horn and pulled herself up. Jack had walked out to almost the same spot where he had watched Mickey work with Missy. It was a good thing to see them together. He had envisioned that they would fit each other and it already appeared to be a great fit. Mickey walked the horse around the corral for twenty minutes, the same corral in which Missy had worked. Jack watching, spoke up.

"Want me to get the gate?"

"Please Jack, would you?"

As he shoved the gate open and backed away, Mickey took no-name through the gap between the corral and the holding pen used for specific animals. She followed a path away from the house, toward the grass of the eastern pasture. It was almost the only large acreage on Two-Jay that hadn't been disked for crops. Jack liked to keep some land fallow, but also available for riding when he wasn't going into town. Step by step, they began learning each other. Quiet for a few miles, Mickey began giving her simple instructions, turning and stopping, all outside the corral now. She even brought her to a lope for about an eighth of a mile. For an hour they learned each other and enjoyed the day in the process. On the way back, she ran into Jack riding Reacher, slowly over the hill toward them. He rode bareback. From two miles separation, they closed on each other at a walk until finally they were abreast each other. Mickey smiled as wide as she could, almost continually. The right man, and an engagement, alongside a new, fine horse and a brand new day. It seemed too much.

"I'm glad you are enjoying no-name," he said. "You look fine on her, really fine. You belong together, anyone can see that.

"And you picked her out for me Jack?" Mickey asked, stroking the reddish hair of her coat in front of the saddle.

"Mostly; I went through about seven horses, all good ones,

until I came to her. She just seemed right. I rode her and finally took Julie with me to get her thoughts."

"And?" Mickey said.

"Julie thought as much of her as I did. She really liked her."

"Jack," Mickey spoke, trying to put it into words. "I know she's a fine horse. I know a lot about horses... and she is fine. She's so very nice! Julie didn't spend too much did she? I know that no-name girl was expensive." She almost felt guilty calling the horse that. But the right name was important. She would find the right one, soon.

"Michaela, Julie loves you a lot. Not only because of me, but because she has...well...fallen in love with you too; in her own way."

"I know, but... was she?" He looked at the horizon as they both sat astride.

"I don't think it's right for me to say. If Julie want's to, she can tell you... but..." He fell silent. You know McKinnets; the next farm down?" Mickey nodded. "You've seen their truck they have, driving back and forth." Again, she nodded.

"Well, that truck is about four years old, and is very nice."

"Yeah?" Mickey tried to follow him, while still rubbing the coat of her new friend. Jack looked at her, waiting. He finally shook his head. He didn't want to talk about it. He didn't want to share what wasn't his to share.

"Yes Jack?" He looked down now and then at her. "About like that truck."

"Oh my gosh! I..." Jack interrupted her thoughts.

"Now look Mickey! I know you wouldn't ever hurt Julie, you wouldn't want to, right?"

"Of course not!" she said, stroking the mane of No-name. He looked at her imploringly.

"Please... just accept No-name, Mickey, Julie wants it that way, okay? Please don't ask anymore." She understood. She did love Julie.

"Done, deal!" Mickey said. She would accept the love she'd been given without more questions.

"Okay, Jack I'll just go with it. I love Julie. Besides, I agreed to keep you out of her kitchen. I have to think about all the ways that I might have at my disposal to do that, so I can keep my word."

"Honey, if you run shy of idea's, I have a few that would keep me out for a long time!" They laughed together. Mickey had never known before what a great healing thing and even a kind of blessing it was to be able to laugh so much.

"But Jack..." she paused, careful to meet him eye to eye. "Thank you for... your part of her."

"Your welcome, honey."

Walking back, sometimes talking, sometimes not, they shared a new day. This was a special day. It was their first day as an engaged couple. Within a half mile of the ranch, she finally spoke again. It was nearing eleven in the morning.

"Jack, when can we see the stars again?"

"As soon as there is a new moon or after. The sky gets really dark then. I'd say about ten days."

"Hmm... what did you call that one star group, the famous one; it started with a Pee?" He thought. "Oh, the Pleiades?" "Yes, that was it. I'd like to see them again." Jack frowned.

"Something wrong?" she asked.

"No, not really, it's just that it was in February when we saw them. Now it's April. The stars, like the moon, rise earlier each night. No big deal, it's just from the rotation of the earth around the sun. But the bottom line is, some of what you see in February, won't be visible by late April. Maybe a little of it in early April, but not late."

They were almost to the ranch. She thought again. "What did you say the names of those seven stars were? The stars of the Pleiades?" He lifted his head, mentally counting.

"Let's see, Alcyone is the brightest. Then Atlas, Electra, Maia, Merope, Taygeta and Pleione. She stopped at the gate. "The third brightest of them was..."

"Electra," he answered. She smiled a full smile, as if she hadn't all day. Then nodding, she stroked the shoulder of the horse, feeling the strength and energy in her.

"Mmm... Yes! I think that seems best. That is a good name for you, girl! "

"Which name?" Jack replied, interested.

"Electra!" I think that will be her name. I'll think about it tonight, but it seems right to me." Jack thought out loud. "Hmm... Electra... Yes that is a great name for a great horse." He smiled at her as he turned Reacher onto the grounds of the ranch. Putting him in the corral to relax, Jack sighed, glad he didn't have a saddle or any of the other gear to mess with today. Mickey slow walked her horse into the barn and to the stall. It had been their first ride. It had been profitable in every way. She seemed to feel comfortable at Two-Jay. They both did. As she removed the bridle and the rest of the gear, she rubbed Electra's body by hand, and then brushed her down. Yes! They both did feel comfortable here. It would be home for both of them.

Hearts

Mickey drove the feed truck over the cattle gate and back onto the house property. All the livestock had been fed while Julie ran the drill this morning, planting the seeds of a new crop in the far field with Jack gone, buying more seed. At twelve-thirty, she took a shower, and put on her city clothes, as she called them now when going to Carson. There still remained enough time to meet the jeweler to discuss a ring for Jack. Four times larger than Redlands, Carson had two jewelers. Confident she would find the right thing for him, she drove with expectation. From Two-Jay, the highway distance, actually drove out to be thirty-three miles to Carson. She made it in twenty-eight minutes. Familiarity with the city in which she was born allowed her to take the shortest route. Parking in front of Crowder's Jewelry, Mickey breathed out a quick sigh. She knew they had what she wanted for Jack. They had to! Amid the glass cases filled with gold, silver and precious stones in all forms, Mickey's anticipation grew. She had gotten a very good price for Missy, and would not forget her.

She now had Julie and Electra, true. But spending a significant amount of money from the sale of her friend and partner, required something as important as a wedding ring. Immediately gravitating to the men's rings, she carefully looked over what the owner, whom her mother knew, had in stock. Everything in the case, while lovely, didn't seem to fit Jack. At the end of the case full of jewelry, she found a gold band about one-quarter inch wide. Perfect for him. Only gold would be appropriate for her kind of love for him.

"Yes, that one!" she said, pointing.

"Oh yes, very nice. The older friend of her mother said. "Fourteen carat and it can be worn it in any environment."

"I'll take it, thank you. And I wonder if you could add something," Mickey asked.

"Certainly!" The gentleman said, encouragingly. "What would you like inscribed?"

"Just one word, please; Hearts!"

J J

Back to Two-Jay in time to get things done on the house, as well as get dinner going for everyone, Mickey found herself joyful. She, in one of those states in a person's life when for a period of time everything seems in balance and aimed in the right direction, also found herself completely contented.

Repeatedly as she worked in the well-equipped, western kitchen, she added one compliment of food to another. Having begun the kitchen work as a help to Julie for the evening meal, before she knew it, the whole thing was done. It had become a western style dinner, like that which everyone ate every day around Redlands. The difference was, that hers today, had grown to five courses and had come about as a by-product of her state of mind. Once the meal was near completion, she turned down the burner and let the main course simmer while walking out to the barn to see her newly named, Electra. Ten minutes spent with her allowed them both to be quiet together. Mickey, trying to get inside the mind of Electra as she had with Missy, watched for signs of bonding and understanding between them. Mickey had always had good communication skills with animals, but particularly horses. She became encouraged by observing the nuances of behavior in Electra until she heard the big tractor. It was the one used for field work. It approaching their home from the direction of the last field to be planted. Its low hum and occasional clang of a towed implement, was unmistakable. When the big motor died down and a door shut, Mickey came from the barn. Seeing Julie, sweaty and tired but confident in her day's work, Julie managed to greet Mickey first.

"Hey Mick! Did you have a good day?"

"The best!" Michaela said, energetically. "I had intended to help you get a few things going for supper, but it kind of got away from me... so we have a complete dinner ready if you can eat my cooking!"

"What? Already done?" Julie leaned back against the tractor that dwarfed her. "What a load off!" she said. "I busted my butt today!" she added, as she reached behind her neck and rubbed. She stood wiping her face with the other hand with a rag from her belt. She looked at Mickey as Mickey qualified the news again.

"I said, if you can eat my cooking, though," she joked. "I'm not the cook you are!"

"Tonight babe, you are one of those thirty-forth or fifty-second street cooks in New York, or whatever street it's on that they have the fancy restaurants. I'm tired!" They walked to the house together as Mickey explained.

"I hope you don't mind but I used some of the venison that you had in the freezer."

"Huh? Oh, that's fine, I'm surprised it was still good. But even if it wasn't, we'll have some mustard sandwiches or something." She smirked.

The wind came up slightly in a gust as they walked to the house together. Almost to the door, Jack came in from the street towing the trailer. They stopped to watch him pull in.

"Looks like he got a few extra things," Julie said. "Well, I'm going in and eat, he can do whatever he wants."

As Julie shut the outer door to the kitchen entrance, Mickey ran to the truck. "Hi Jack! Your day go okay?" He smiled at her. "Just fine, kitten; a little tired though."

"Well, Julie just got back and I told her that I have dinner ready for you two. So come in and eat when you are ready."

"Right behind you, kitten." She took his arm as he stepped slow and tired toward the house. "What's this kitten thing about? You've never called me that before?"

"Huh? Oh... well, nothing really, I just was thinking a lot about you today, and your soft, round tail."

"Uhh-huh!" she said, slapping him on the back and pushing him through the doorway, into the kitchen.

Walking in and dropping his handful of receipts on the counter by the door, he stopped short at the smell of the kitchen. Just as he breathed in deeply the smell of the southwestern dinner, Julie came around the corner of the hallway from the bathroom.

"Hey Jack! Look at what Mick has done for dinner. I came home a little early thinking I was going to have to cook, since she'd said she would be gone today. And this is what I found!"

"It's not all that!" Mickey began apologetically. "Just some things I threw together." Julie bent to taste the main course over a large cooking skillet. She dipped the wooden spoon into the mix twice, tasting it each time.

"Okay, that is about the best thing I've ever eaten. Where did you pick that up?" Julie asked.

"Oh, things you learn, you know."

Jack moved close to taste the venison mixed with a small amount of beef and a large amount of beans in a southwest sauce. "Mickey, I keep finding things out about you. You said you didn't cook much." But she corrected him. "I said I hadn't cooked much these last years; because at that time I had Missy." Jack looked at Julie, then back at the stove. He tasted it and sat down the cook spoon. "Hmm.. let me get washed up real quick and we'll give it the real test."

Reasonably clean, each of them sat to a supper of the southwestern stew-fry, with rolls, homemade tortilla chips, salad and lemon bars for dessert.

"Wow Mick! This was worth getting up for and working all day! Maybe when we're busy like this you could do it again," Julie said emphatically. It was as much a statement as it was a question.

"Of course! I kind of like cooking, but I don't want to move in on your territory. After all, I agreed to keep Jack out of the kitchen. It's hard to do that when I'm *in* the kitchen." Julie ate another bite of the entree.

"Well, it's like this sister... if you cook like this, I'll find something for lover boy to do to keep his mind off you!" She slurped slightly as she ate. I don't know, cleaning the toilet, maybe." They laughed, enjoying the dinner and time together. Jack ignored her at first as he ate, then spoke.

244

"Aww Julie, you have that special way of making a man feel loved!"

Julie examined the home made tortilla chips and shook her head. "Excellent," she said quietly, her thoughts escaping her lips. "Uhh-huh," she said in reply to Jacks ribbing her.

"When Jack?" Julie said. He looked up at her in response.

"When what?" he said flatly, wiping his mouth.

"When's the wedding? I mean, you got this girl here so happy and all engaged up like she is... you just going to leave her hanging until you draw social security, or what?" Jack dropped his fork into his plate.

"Honestly Julie, it was only nine months ago or something like that, when you were trying to set me up with Sally Mae Somebody who had just decided to go into the cattle business. We were all down at the steak house having a meal and you pestered me all the way home. So look, I found Mickey all by myself, and I pulled my underwear on by myself that day too, believe it or not! And every day since. I took her out and we walked and talked and everything. Plus maybe a few things you don't know about. I EVEN KISSED HER BY MYSELF! I think I got it, okay? I can bring it home from here! Are you planning on a honeymoon together, the three of us? Are you going to be peekin' in our room to make sure I'm doing things right? You know, to make sure that we have a chance of having that little niece of yours? Really Julie! One more word from you and I'm telling Mike at the CO-OP that he's first in the running for the BREED WITH JULIE, contest."

Julie stared at him absently, as if he was speaking German.

"I see..." she said blankly, turning to Mickey who had come to love the war of words between her man and her sister. "Mick, when you're ready, you tell him what you want. If he doesn't get with it, we'll use a hot-shot on him." Jack, now irritated, reached across the aisle to the counter and picked up his phone, staring at his sister. "You really don't think I'll call Mike do you?" It seemed to solve the issue, until the last lemon bar was gone.

Michaela watched Jack at the table. In her mind she instinctively knew that no one is perfect, but in her heart she didn't want to acknowledge that. He came as close as anyone she had known. A hard day's work for the Gentners and a day spent planning and cooking for Mickey; followed by a delicious meal left each of them contented and resistant to get up from the table. Each was thinking to themselves until Mickey spoke.

"What about Saturday Jack?" He looked at her, half-awake now, contented from the meal.

"Saturday for what? he replied, leaning back and stretching out enough under the table to kick Julie's boot.

"To get married! What do you think?"

It was as if both Jack and Julie were watching a tennis match from opposite sides of the court, both turning their heads in unison to stare at Mickey who was the ball. Not believing what she had said, he sat up. "What brought this on?" he asked. She now had his full attention.

"I was just thinking. If I heard you right earlier, you about have the disking and drilling done as far as you want to go; and you said that the stars were best with the new moon." He was confused. "Sure, I said that, but what's that got to do with getting married Saturday?"

"See, if we get married Saturday, we'll be able to see the stars. I would like to get married under the night sky Jack. We could have a wedding in the church, with a few candles, but how would that be compared to ten thousand stars as candles around us. As long as the minister could be on the hill with us, I would love it! So, what do you think?" Jack sat still, digesting what Mickey had asked. In his organized, methodical way of doing things, he tried to come up with an objection. But the truth was, he was also a romantic. It showed in nearly everything he did. Evident in his love of the prairie and the night sky, he was too much of one in fact! And there was just enough of it in him to make the difference. He stared at the crumbles of lemon bar on his plate.

"I guess, we could... if you want."

Mickey couldn't hold back her excitement. She jumped from her chair and hugged him.

"I know it's sudden Jack, but we've got five days to work on it."

Thinking he had to offer a thought, he spoke.

"We don't have clothes or anything, honey."

"Maybe we do... let's clean up the dishes and then we can talk about it."

♩ ♩

The week went by opposite to what Mickey expected. She had thought it would be a rush, a whirlwind. And though the few important things that needed attention drew it, On the whole, it was an hour-by-hour preparation with little things thought through, and big things looked forward to; it was best that way. She even found time each day to stand and talk with Electra, moving her into the open corral or even taking a short ride once. Julie would help with cooking. There would be no guests since it was so near, but there would be a party next month, and the hundreds of people who knew Jack and Julie would come to that gathering. Evenings were spent together, the three of them for most of the evening. Following that, the two of them in the den, hallway, or talking in one of their bedrooms, before a fitful sleep in their own rooms with their own thoughts.

Friday came, no earlier or later than any other day, but Mickey was up before dawn, saddling Electra. They would go out together for an hour or so, in the cool morning of mid-April. She thought as she rode silently. Whatever is missed between this morning and tomorrow night, won't be needed. Everything that is

248

remembered will be kept. And everything kept, treasured.

They stepped into the morning and onto the pasture, east of home. She rode southeast at a walk for twenty minutes before reaching the lower areas of the fields in this corner of Two-Jay. Fog, a ground cloud had formed in the bottom of the lower land. Hundreds of yards wide, the mist was cool to her face as they rode into it. Electra seemed to enjoy the opaque air as much as Mickey did. It energized her. Mickey nudged Electra into a lope, plunging them into the dim morning cloud heading away from the ranch, then turning back toward home, repeating the play again and again. It was a moment for them to bond, within the cloud. Twenty minutes later, their minds and hearts alive with inspiration, they headed back on a slow walk home.

While standing in the barn removing the bit and bridle with the rest, Jack walked into the barn and stepped up behind her as she lightly stroked the bridge of Electra's nose.

"You love her, don't you?"

"More than I can say," she replied, surrounded by the smells of damp dirt and floating dust that are always present in a stable. "We just had the time of our lives. I can't thank you and Julie enough," she smiled, as he returned it.

"Still good for tomorrow night?" he asked, relieved that they didn't have to have a large wedding. Still, a small part of him wondered if she would regret not having one. She turned to him with a half-smile. He melted from it.

"Unless you want out mister!" she said. He reached to her and held her without words for minutes. He could smell her hair, just as he had the day of their picnic, seven months before. Then he replied. "There is an old Spanish proverb that goes like this... *a man who has loved one woman, has loved them all. A man who has loved many women, has loved none at all. You...* are my one." Silently Michaela cried. She had been so much more emotional since the hospital. She felt the same. It would be a perfect wedding, no matter what. She knew that. It wouldn't be a show, nor any kind of production. It would hold all the meaning it should.

J J

Saturday was as she had hoped, not busy and worrisome like many brides on their wedding day. She had determined to keep fussiness to a minimum. They knew each other well. They knew how each other thought, and about each other's goals and dreams. She was at peace with it all.

Jack spent the morning in Redlands for a few last details. He received a few happy greetings from the few friends whom he knew who had heard of his marriage to Michaela. One had been from the elevator. Walking by the hardware store on his way down Main Street, Jack waved into the front window. He always waved. Though difficult to tell from the street at the moment, if there was anyone on the inside to wave back, he waved anyway.

It was habit. Pete, a young boy whom he had known in Redlands, almost since he was born, saw him and ran out the front door, catching Jack on the street.

"Whatchasay Jack!" The boy offered him a high-five. Jack, in such a high mood, put extra effort in it today. Uncharacteristically, Jack spun around and gave Pete the high-five on the return rotation. He waited, taking time to talk with him.

"Hey Pete! You okay today?"

"I'm vanishing Jack... moving so fast today that I haven't had time to pee!" Jack laughed at the kid's phrase.

"Working hard huh?"

"Yes sir, Jack. And I want you to know that I myself, plus my mom appreciate you helping me get this job here! It has made such a difference in mom's...um... days, ya know?" Jack looked at him closer. "I guess, so?" he said.

"Well, you know dad passed away last year." Jack nodded somberly. He did indeed remember the father of the young teen. "Well, since you helped me get work here by talking to Mr. Wuster, I have been able to help mom with the bills and do a few fun things for myself besides!" I'll never forget what you did for us Jack!" On Main Street, in front of the hardware store, on a Saturday morning; the morning of the day in which he would be married, Jack put his arm around Pete, and gave him solid support and affection. He held him close, longer than he thought he would. "That's great Pete! You are a hard worker! Mr. Wuster has told me that. I'm proud of you! Anytime that you have time, come out to Two-Jay and you can go for a ride on Reacher."

"Aw Jack, that would be smash and grab!" Jack laughed out loud and took the phrase to mean that the boy would like to take advantage of the offer. He stood smiling at Pete.

"Anyway thanks, Jack. I guess that's all I wanted. Just to tell you thanks and that I won't let you down for taking a chance on me." This time, Jack stood straight and held out his hand to Pete. Pete was young, but he was a man. As Pete, wiped his hand off on his jeans to clean it, he stood straight and shook Jack's hand. Jack turned to walk away as he smiled at Pete. The proud friend of one of the nicest guys in town he felt, watched him walk down the street. He wanted to be like him one day.

"See ya Jack, if I can ever do anything to help you, you just holler, Okay?" Jack stopped, turned and walked back to Pete slowly. Pete hung onto the open door of the store.

"You know, Pete, there is one thing you could do that would help me..."

Michaela spent her day for the most part in planning small things for the evening, the night and tomorrow. Some time she spent going over the little things, the small details. But Jack handled a lot of that. The simple marriage license that the minister would give them, showing evidence of the ceremony would be all Jack would require. After that, it would be an evening under the stars on a small hill on Two-Jay. Having

252

decided on such short notice to be married on this day, he had hoped all week that the weather would cooperate.

At one p.m. Jack sat at the kitchen table looking outward at the grounds and the sky. Throughout the day, each crossed paths, and traded comments. And they ate. Snacks in the kitchen for everyone to grab, made it handy. It should be a fine night, he thought as he looked out at the sky. They would use Julie's "traveling truck', which she almost never drove. Comfortable, with a topper on it to keep warmth inside, he also had a small heater that could be run from a quiet generator, twenty feet away if they needed it. It would be a novel wedding for sure. He had heard of people being married on mountains, in the air on parachutes, even underwater. But a wedding at night, under the stars was a unique thought to him. He was amazed that she had thought of it, but happy too. He remembered the cold night in February when they stood huddled together in the seeming sanctity of space and clear air with ten thousand stars of the Milky Way above them. He agreed with her that it had been the nicest night of his life. "Up to this point, anyway." He laughed out the words, wishing for the romance to be present in their truck bed-bed. He knew her well. He knew she had considered that. And it was okay.

It was a short ceremony, but meaningful. It had become what she wanted, and what he wanted. No pretense, no production value; only love. Jack wore his best jeans and shirt with his best seven-ex hat. He also wore his new boots, the ones she had bought for him. Mickey wore a fine country dress, even if for less than an hour. As he thanked their minister for traveling all the way back into the hills of his property with Julie, Jack tried to take in the moment. Julie had served as a bride's maid. Pete, his young friend from the hardware store, a boy of fourteen; who had taken a liking to Jack every time he was in town for the last two years, was best man. They had become friends. And Pete shared Jack's joy this night. He had lost his father. That was something Jack understood. It had been a way for Pete to give back to the six-foot, relaxed cowboy that he had come to like so well, like most people in Redlands. The only other witness, was Pete's mother. Jack had known her in a limited way from their lives in Redlands. Nearly everyone knew everyone in Redlands.

Jack smiled, just to himself now. There were hugs and small discussions behind him, where he stood in the near darkness. He looked out over Two-Jay. Not much was visible in the darkness. A few distant lights shined far on the horizon. They were the only ones high enough at the ranch to be seen from here. In his best seven-x Stetson, he laughed to himself now at the thought that by Sunday evening, nearly everyone in Redlands would know that they had spent the night in the bed of a truck on a hill in the dark at the ranch. Julie would see to that. He was sure of it. As the farm truck engine came to life behind him, he turned around waving. The light inside of the cab was on, and Julie waved a meaningful wave of congratulations to him, to them. Within a minute, everyone was gone. There was little sound. The wind whispered through the stand of high blackjack oak fifty yards away, much as it had that day in October when they were first here. She held his hand in the darkness. He stared into nothing and thought of what a road it had been. Nervous, funny, work... and reward.

For an hour, they said nothing. They didn't need to. Heart to heart, they stood as they had stood in February when cold. He held her from behind, arms wrapped around her. With lifted heads they shared the stars. Before moving from where they stood, she asked the names of a few of the stars over their heads. Filling in the blanks for her, she breathed in deep and turned around to hug him.

"Jack... you know so much!" she said in a whisper as he held her in the quiet.

"Not enough... there is never time to know everything," he said. Michaela nudged him in the ribs.

"Hey cowboy, want to know me?" she kidded in the darkness that hid her face.

"I thought you'd never ask," he said, as he grabbed her hungrily. They stood, Jack kissing her beneath the tall trees, in the tall grass which had remained over winter. As the latch shut on the topper of Julie's truck, they slipped beneath the pile of blankets that lay inside. There, on a small hill in the wide plains of North America, sat in the darkness of night, a pickup truck that couldn't be seen. And on the license plate, also not seen in the darkness, it simply said "Two-Jay."

Rodeo

The day of the local rodeo came with a flair. Everyone they knew was there if they could get away from responsibilities. He saw many of them as they passed through the crowds. Mickey, had given the tickets she'd bought to Julie, who had planned on taking a friend, though neither she nor Jack had seen her.

A rodeo is unlike any other sporting event. Wherever one looked, it was a scene. Thousands of boots, thousands of cowboy hats. Even ranchers Jack knew well who normally wore ball caps to do their ranching or farm work were there at the local rodeo in their best five-ex or seven-ex cowboy hats. Jeans and belt buckles were everywhere; some as large as Texas. Some were in the shape of Texas. Everyone in the area with an interest in rodeo, was there. It had only been little more than a one hour drive to today's rodeo from Two-Jay.

Jack listened as the announcer spoke with pride about the famous rodeos of the industry.

"With a large Cowboy association containing thousands competitors nationally in a circuit, by the time these work worn cowboys and cowgirls have completed a season, there are only a little over one-hundred competitors left for a national title rodeo each year. The biggest and most well-known rodeos throughout the United States each year, are scattered throughout the country. Not merely in the west. While Oregon, California and Nevada are home to many famous rodeos, Utah and Wyoming are part of the rodeo circuit and famous for celebrations that can last days. Many famous or frontier rodeos gather hundreds of thousands of spectators! Some of the country's large outdoor rodeos begin or end with celebrations, western style! Some began in the 1800's and many rodeos feature community events each year. Parades and concerts, air shows and hundreds of thousands or even close to a million in prize money! Some celebrations can last up to a week! Many rodeos you will remember your whole life! Events, some with dances and Native American exhibits surround the rodeo with fun. Most contestants work toward these or other large rodeos throughout the country which are also found in the North, East and Southern U.S. But Reno, Cheyenne, Dodge City, and Rapid City are also a big draw out here in the West!"

The biggest rodeo, the pinnacle of the rodeo industry, had been held in Oklahoma for longer than Jack had been alive. But for local fun, easy access and seeing the beginnings of the season, the local rodeos are just as enjoyable. As they walked, hand in hand and soul in soul, in the truest sense, Mickey and Jack enjoyed their newfound state as lovers and spouses, but not the least of all, as friends. For both of them it had been perfect. It was new, it was clean and it was good. It was everything both had dreamed. It was a good day. And a good day at the rodeo.

A top-notch Quarter Horse pony was being given away as a prize. Jack had never seen that happen before. It was a first! The chestnut color of the pony and good breeding made the contest to win it a big draw. Even Jack entered. Hot dogs and Hamburgers fed most of the crowd. The Bronc Busters, Bull Riders and Calf Ropers were, as all those who climb mountains or fight wars, heavy with the experience. The elation of winning the battle or the dejection of a lost chance taken, which could never be recovered was felt in the air with each event.

All the while the cheers went on as if it was a boxing match or a baseball game. One by one, each of the contestants received their scores and where they ranked in each competition. The winners were determined by the total of prize money earned. It is always the sprains, broken bones and wounded pride that were common at these events which determined the survivors. Mickey, as excited as Jack at some of the events she had never seen, cheered. The eight seconds of a bull ride were brutal, often requiring days, weeks or even months to recuperate from for some of the riders. The steers weighing around seventeen-hundred pounds were a natural to the action and danger. This is rodeo. It was as different as one could get from the precise and methodical movements and accolades that she had experienced in equitation. For a moment she missed

Missy deeply. But it had been the right thing to do. She took a deep breath sitting down next to three people who were eating. Most were sharing a hot dog. Then sharing the mustard that inevitably became smeared on lips and faces and gave excuse for kisses with the best of memories. Jack, biting on an extra-long hot dog, smeared with too much mustard, chewed one bite for the full length of the eight second bull ride of a cowboy from his county. Many were from Texas. Just as many were from Oklahoma, Kansas or other western states. As he ate and watched the elimination of riders, Mickey watched him. Between each bite of each cylindrical sandwich, she remembered a special time they had. Each buzzer that sounded, each round of cheers at the end of an event, matched her own heart in the winning of life and love.

Jack pointed out the dangers of each event, along with what he knew of each contestants capabilities. Dangers in rodeo, like health and love, were many. But it was always worth the effort for the winner. A long break between events allowed them to walk the grounds and see the vendors, hawkers and each business that maintained their livelihood from the rodeo circuit. People usually attended the rodeo from all states. From time to time he would see ranchers he knew, who congratulated him on his marriage and met Mickey with a smile and a handshake. Like the smell of hay and dirt, the smell of livestock was everywhere. With them, long trailers and pickups littering the lots for parking. Ironically, the ease of navigating the area on horse was far preferable to trying to drive a vehicle through the maze.

After a full morning and part afternoon, the excitement of the wins of their personal favorites was balanced with the I-told-you-so of those who had been favored but lost. Jack found the ticket stubs in his pocket as he looked for a note he carried, to meet a friend. Relaxing during a break at two p.m., Jack and Michaela stood outside the arena and visited with passing friends, old and new. From time to time a female voice would call out with a clear "Hello Jack!" as a previous friend of the six-foot cowboy from Two-Jay. He pulled out the short stubs from his pocket and gazed at their used tickets. Remembering the day he had bought them in an impulsive preparation for a date with her, he took satisfaction at his efforts to win her heart. He had caught himself before throwing the tickets away. He would keep them, frame them and remember this day as part of their honeymoon, an important part. He would remember it as part of his personal rodeo of soul and body with the winners and losers. His eyes squinted as he laughed when Mickey poked him in the ribs, asking what he was thinking.

"Just remembering when I bought these for you," he said, showing her the stubs.

"You had bought your own, and we joked about that on the way to our first picnic."

In the midst of the throngs of people arriving, those leaving, hot dog buyers, hat buyers and the occasional dejected contestant passing by in clothes that had been changed, Michaela leaned onto his chest. Heart thankful for obtaining her wishes and dreams in life, this; all of it, could never in her mind be termed sappy. It could never be remembered as anything except winning in life. As she leaned into him, he smelled her hair again, just as he had on that day at the picnic. He held her hand in his, firmly, closely. It was a reward for a love that been saved for the person of his dreams. Though he had experienced opportunity after opportunity to settle in various degrees, he had always wanted the best. He had been patient. He had worked hard, endured the unexpected, bitter winters, dry summers, low bankbooks, broken equipment and waitresses with too many screws loose; and he had won. He had won in work, won in life, won in the wife of his dreams. He had won against all the things that others had said were too elusive, or foolish to chase. He had won.

As Michaela excused herself to the cowgirl's room with a pat on his chest and a promise to return soon, he stood back close to a wall and watched the crowd. Sunlight fell in shafts of light through the overhead windows of the outer promenade of the arena. He caught a glimpse through the crowd of a beautiful woman in a rodeo shirt and short skirt. Her red and white western shirt with fringe on it, like western lace, seemed alive with her movements. Her legs in the short, matching skirt were drawing the attention of several men as she spoke with another girl. He couldn't see her face. She had turned away from him with her head shielded by a white, costume cowgirl hat, tipped back on her head. He stood admiring a kind of feminine familiarity of her as he waited. The crowds of people and rush of movement kept him from hearing her conversation with the other woman. But he was sure he knew her. As he thought, a strong hand grabbed him by the shoulder.

"Jack! My friend, how have you been?" Taken by surprise by the strong grip and instantly renewed memories, he shook Dean Chance's hand. Within minutes, they had caught up on personal history and shared the experiences of each other over the previous three years. Having lived near Two-Jay and Redlands ten years before; and still not married, he sincerely congratulated Jack in his success with his own. The six-foot one-inch man with a strong, driving personality and a preference for a good tussle and competition in his zeal for life, answered Jack's returned questions.

"Naw, Jack! I just haven't found the right woman! Darn it! Here I am, thirty-five and I've got a good ranch, but I've gotta' have a lively woman. That's a must! You know what I mean, not a little prima-donna. I need a woman to give me a run for my money, ya' know?" As Jack listened to him over the crowd noise and the announcer notifying the crowd of the next event, Jack heard a familiar laugh. As he turned back to look, the woman was still there, talking with the other girl, and being admired by passing men. Some of the men were real, working cowboys and some merely wannabes. They were all however unashamedly admiring her bare, beautiful legs. He visually followed them downward from the skirt she wore until they disappeared into her fancy red and white boots with stars embroidered on them. As Dean kept describing his ideal of womanhood, Jack suddenly stopped cold. He saw the woman's face! DING! It was like the dinner bell of Pavlov's dog. It was perfect! Jack touched the taller man's arm with a finger. "Just a minute Dean... don't leave! He smiled a full smile. It was his best, most convincing smile, as he called out to her. "Hey Julie! Come here a minute...there is someone I want you to meet!"

Acknowledgment

I wish to thank my wife Connie for her valuable contributions on the chapter Grade 'A'. Her experience and insight has been strengthening.